CW00967891

MICHAEL GLENNON

HARDBOILED BOOKS

Song and Dance

Michael Glennon

ISBN (Print Edition): 979-8-35098-567-2

ISBN (eBook Edition): 979-8-35098-568-9

Cover design by Jason A. Berry

ONE

He's Gone

My uncle James, my mother's younger brother, barely survived the sixties, but before he dropped down a rabbit hole, he bequeathed me his sound system and extensive record collection. Thus, my musical taste runs a generation behind, so, to no surprise, I was tuned to an oldies station while on my way to meet a prospective client. Also unsurprisingly, I picked up an earworm, and the whole time I sat listening to Elizabeth Taft Gardner run on about her missing husband, the Rascals' *It's a Beautiful Morning* was looping through my brain. Sadly, I wouldn't be on my way, enjoying the brand-new day, till I knew the job was mine. My bank account was running on empty, and I needed the work.

"Have you ever handled a missing person's case before, Mr. Rotten?" my prospective client was asking me, as her friend, Alison Owen, paced behind her in the Gardners' tastefully appointed and relentlessly color-coordinated living room.

"Certainly," I bluffed, though it wasn't an outright lie. One of my first clients had been a deranged cross-dresser who hired me to find his recovering ex-wife—recovering from drug addiction brought on by his abuse. Only he hadn't worn a skirt to our first meeting, and he never mentioned that he was divorced from said "wife," or out on parole, or under a restraining order. And he hadn't mentioned the abuse, only the drugs. Not surprisingly, the case had not ended well. He nearly cut her throat, and I never got paid, but she *had* been lost, and I *had* helped find her. My conscience was clear.

"But even in a city the size of Pittsburgh," I continued, "People like your husband don't disappear every day." Malodorous poor folk, perhaps, but not sweet-smelling, consummately privileged suburbanites. No, this place smelled like money, fussy upper-middle-class money. Rich money doesn't care what it smells like, and poverty stinks. The Gardners had enough of the green stuff to eliminate odors and design away conflict, but not enough *not* to care what other people thought. Professional decorator, cleaning woman, plant service. Very sober nineties.

"Has your husband ever done anything like this before?" I asked to nudge her from the subject of my credentials. Mister Missing had taken a casino excursion to Atlantic City over the previous weekend but missed the bus back.

"More like, 'How many times,'" said Alison who continued to pace protectively behind her friend.

"Allie, please," said Ms. Liz, sitting stiffly.

My new client was attractive enough, in a mature, soccer-mom sort of way, but her lanky brunette buddy was a true head-turner and proving to be a serious distraction. I had to remind myself that the rent was due and concentrate on the business at hand.

"Billy has taken tours before, to gamble. It's his way of relaxing," the distraught wife said. "But he's always come back. He wouldn't miss school . . ." she added and then trailed off. She tried, but couldn't finish, and spent a moment sniffling. The wayward husband was a teacher at the local elementary school.

"I don't know why you're even looking for the worthless bastard," fumed her friend with brown eyes flashing. "Let him stay lost."

"Alison, go smoke a cigarette," said Elizabeth with an edge in her voice.

Allie frowned, but dutifully departed, and Liz seemed to settle once she was out of the room.

"You two having any money trouble?" I asked after she had wiped her nose.

"Billy and me? No," she said without elaboration.

"Any marital difficulties? Other women? Other men?" I asked as delicately as I could, although I have to admit that delicacy is not my strong suit.

She looked momentarily confused. "No," she finally said with a trace of annoyance.

"Your husband subject to depression? Under a doctor's care? Any alcohol or drug dependency?"

"Billy drinks socially, but he doesn't do drugs," she said. "He wasn't too thrilled about turning forty, but there's nothing unusual about that."

"No, I suppose not." *Certainly not for some self-absorbed, yuppie thumb-sucker*, I thought to myself before adding, "How about at work? Any problems with the principal?"

"Billy never talks much about his work, but he's been at the same school for ten years, so I don't think he was having any problems," she said and paused. "I told them he has the flu."

This woman had a problem. She'd gotten too used to tap dancing around the truth to be of any help in finding her husband. He might be rotting in the basement for all she was willing to admit. I was ready to take up smoking and join the tart-tongued temptress on the porch.

"I appreciate the confidence you have in me," I said, which was a joke, since she'd let her fingers do the walking and found my name in the phone book, "But this type of investigation is best handled by the police."

"Unfortunately, the police have been no help at all," she said. "They have no discretion whatsoever. They won't do a thing unless I file an official report, and if I do, they'll march straight into the principal's office."

I made a mental note to send a dozen donuts to the local precinct house.

"Ms. Gardner, I gotta level with you," I said without a trace of shame. "If your husband's in hiding, he could be difficult to flush out. And if something's happened to him, the police would be notified. Hiring me is a long shot. I can poke around, maybe travel down there, but if I don't find a lead in a few days, the police would be in a better position to follow-up." I let that sink in and then finished with, "I'll need a five-hundred-dollar advance."

She nodded her acceptance. What choice did she have? She had enough money to hire somebody better so she must have had her reasons for turning to someone like me. I didn't press further, but I did tell her some background info might help, and she led me to a spare bedroom which Billy Boy had converted to a home office.

"Your husband goes on these bus tours with any of his friends?" I asked as I surveyed the absent man's effects.

She thought a moment. "I guess he doesn't have any real friends, at least that I know of."

Miz Liz seemed uncomfortable in her husband's room, and I got the impression she hadn't come in here that often. She suggested I talk to Phil Cheswick, the guy who ran the bus tours, and she gave me the name of one of Billy's teaching colleagues I could approach without arousing suspicion. Then, mercifully, a phone rang, and she left to answer it. I heard the beginnings of two heated exchanges before a heavy door closed, and I was left alone in the room which Billy Gardner had called his own. This room, at least, had some personality. But whose? The atmosphere was more Late Sixties Dorm Room than Contemporary Professional Study. Regrettably, I'd seen many of this guy's most-prized possessions for sale at flea markets and yard sales, or on those cheesy, late-night TV commercials. Classic rock CD reissues by brain-dead bands of thirty years ago mixed with well-thumbed works by Carlos Castaneda and Hermann Hesse. A tape of James Taylor's performance with the Boston Pops from Public TV sat beside membership info from politically correct organizations like the Sierra Club and Common Cause. A poorly focused photo of Bad Bill with hair to his shoulders sported the caption, "The times they are a-changin'." Wow. I bet they bought a piece of Clinton's campaign and sat around on election night congratulating themselves for saving the world. Is it safe?

A desk was stacked with papers awaiting grades, but no notes to himself and nothing that looked like a diary or a secret address book. There were books on gambling mixed with borderline New Age philosophy. There were framed photos that appeared to be stills from old black-and-white TV shows, and there were two framed tickets to the first Woodstock music festival. None of which gave me any idea of where this guy might be, although some suggested where he was coming from. Dreams die hard.

"Do you have a stamp?" asked my new boss from the doorway as she presented the slip of paper I'd been waiting for.

"Just make it out to 'Frank Rotten.' I left my stamp at the office," I lied.

Ms. Liz had composed herself, but her blazing cheeks revealed the effort. I wouldn't have minded seeing Allie again, but I wanted to depart before becoming part of the problem. I pocketed my advance, promised daily updates, smiled warmly, and took my leave.

TWO

It's Money That Matters

I'm not ashamed to admit that money was mainly on my mind. My landlord, a hedonistic, self-proclaimed artist, who declined to sell his art and went by the singular name of Rodolfo, was throwing another of his killer studio parties that weekend. If I was late with the rent, my invitation would be rescinded. I was so focused on finding a branch of Allegheny National so I could deposit my first payday in weeks, that I almost missed the pearl gray Phantom that seemed to be shadowing me along the winding suburban lane. Such a luxury car was slightly out of place in that neighborhood, but the Rolls rolled straight after I turned into the Aspinwall Mini-Mall, and I didn't give it a second thought.

After depositing my check, I found myself almost at the door of Cheswick Travel, home of Shore Tours, which put together my missing man's casino excursion. I hesitated. I hadn't planned to start work right away. I wanted to call my roommate and be sure he still had his half of the rent. My priorities were well-established, but I didn't often get an advance, and I tend to confuse coincidence with fate, so I parked my battered wagon and went fishing for Phil Cheswick.

Cheswick Travel was a typical strip mall storefront operation. The outer door opened into a holding pen with half-a-dozen hard plastic chairs and a table cluttered with resort displays. Canned tuneage leaked from unseen speakers. Two institutional desks stretched side-by-side across the center of the room, and there was a semi-private, glass-walled sanctuary in the rear. Behind one of the big desks sat a gum-cracking receptionist.

I asked for information about casino excursions and was handed a brochure. I asked to see Phil Cheswick and was told he was attending a travel seminar in town. Best time to catch the boss was in the early afternoon. Phil's Gal Friday did not want to know if there was anything she could do to help. She wanted to return to her fashion zine, and even though I was on the edge of irritation, she was kinda cute, and I let her off the hook. Mañana, mañana. I vowed to return.

Not an auspicious start. It occurred to me as I walked to my car that I didn't know what the hell I was doing, but I attributed my ill humor to lack of nourishment and set off in search of a Taco Bell. That I knew I could find. A Chicken Burrito Supreme and cup of black coffee later, I decided to call my friend and neighbor, Trudy Bonner. Trudy was my benchmark, my sounding board, and occasional co-conspirator. The poor girl still worked for the same spirit-sucking insurance company that had sacked me eleven months earlier. I'd helped her get the job, and she showed her gratitude now by providing access to the company's data banks and background services. I figured it couldn't hurt to have DMV and credit checks run on my new clients.

"You took five hundred dollars of that poor woman's money?" she said in disbelief after I'd sketched the scene.

"Totally, Trude. I told you this gig would start paying off some-day. And she's not poor. I may get more. She's got quite the nice set up."

"Frank, you can't handle a missing person's case. The last one got her throat cut." Trudy had helped me find the recovering ex-wife by searching through police reports. A tedious chore but somebody had to do it.

"C'mon, Trude. That was just a scratch. It didn't even need stitches. No way could I have seen it coming. This is totally different. Strictly legit."

"What if this guy's lying around dead somewhere?"

"If he's dead, what difference does it make who's looking for him? She's already been to the police, but she won't file an offi-cial report 'cause she wants to keep a lid on things."

"What if he's half-dead?" she asked perversely. "You're out of your league, Frank."

"Hey, girl, thanks for the vote of confidence. If you don't want to help, I'll corrupt one of your co-workers," I said, which was a total bluff since she was the only one of my ex-associates who would still speak to me. "I swear no screw-ups this time. I'm going straight to the library to do some research."

Lucky for me, Trudy couldn't stand my whining. I promised to drop by her place later with a complete report, and she finally agreed to have something for me by the end of the next day.

THREE

Takin' Care of Business

I didn't get much respect, and I guess it wasn't hard to see why. I'd been in business almost a year and was still operating on a shoestring. I didn't have a real office—just a desk in the corner of the living room where I set up my answering machine and sorted my mail. "The city is my office," I used to tell people—friends— though I never admitted as much to clients. I'd tell *them* I'd be happy to come to their office or home, or, if they wanted to keep a low profile, I'd suggest a clandestine meeting in the lobby of a big hotel downtown.

I spent a lot of time on the road, so I kept a lot of stuff in my car, an old Toyota wagon, and maintained a mental list of climate-controlled retreats with rest room facilities. I knew all the Mickey D's and diners around town, even though they were always crowded around lunch time. Bus terminals and municipal buildings had their uses, but their clientele was questionable. Libraries were good, as long as you steered clear of the children's section. People assume you're a pervert if you read picture books and don't have kids. College libraries were especially good. Anyone with a driver's license can get a card at any one of the state university libraries, and most of those have reciprocal agreements with private schools. Wherever I go, I act like I know what I'm doing, and I always wear a tie. You can do almost anything you want in this town if you wear a tie while you're doing it.

Scene investigations are my bread and butter. Which car was where at the point of impact and who had the stop sign. That sort of stuff. ("There, ya see that spot where the bark is off the tree? That's where the asshole went into the woods.") I'd do eight or ten a week for sleazeball contingency attorneys at fifty bucks a pop. That was usually enough to pay the bills and feed my face. Gigs like this missing person case were gravy, and it was gravy I needed to get ahead. To really establish myself, I'd have to have a video camera, a smoked-glass surveillance van, and sophisticated software so I could generate my own credit reports and DMV checks. Maybe I'd even hire an assistant to do some of the leg work. In the meantime, I couldn't afford to be without Trudy's help, so I crossed the river and swung down to the library at Pitt where I hoped to develop a plan of attack. The main drawback with working at college libraries is you can waste entirely too much time scoping co-eds. Twenty minutes after sitting down in the periodicals room, I was still staring at a blank sheet of notebook paper. Total babes all around, tossing their hair, chewing their pencils, chatting with friends. Even baggy clothes didn't help. I'm too good at mental undressing. I was ready to re-enroll until I had a vision of myself trying to explain to Trudy what I'd done with my afternoon. I gave myself a mental smack to the head and wondered what I was trying to accomplish. In life, with this case, whatever.

Obviously, I was trying to find Billy Gardner, but I was also trying to make a living without working too hard. Like everybody else, right? I figured the advance would cover three six-hour days plus expenses if I stayed around Pittsburgh. And if I wrapped this thing up by Saturday, I wouldn't have to hammer my client for additional funds, *and* I could still make it to Rodolfo's party. If Miz Liz insisted that I travel to America's Playground, then I'd revise my plan. The way I saw it, either something nasty had happened to this guy, or he just flaked out. Random acts of violence are not as common as Americans make them out to be, and bodies don't just disappear, except for Jimmy Hoffa's, so I had to assume Billy Boy was off somewhere on his own. He could be having marital problems, maybe a mid-life crisis, or he could be driven by some compulsive behavior, like gambling. I could easily understand how relations might be strained with a frozen fish like Miz Liz, but the idea of a hippy-dippy gambling guy didn't add up, unless there was something subversive about placing bets that I was missing. Nathan Detroit had his charm, but I could never fathom the pull some people feel for laying a wager. I like the idea of easy money as much as the next guy, but life is risky enough without escalating the elements of chance. Besides, what more could Wayward William want? He had the wife, the job, the house, and a nice assortment of expensive toys—what was he missing?

What was I missing? Background, maybe? Since I was in the periodicals room, I scanned the index for articles on gambling and was amazed at the amount of recent activity. You could legally lose your shirt at racetracks, on river boats, on barges, in churches, and on Indian reservations. For law-breaking traditionalists, there were the numbers runners and betting pools of organized crime. Every neighborhood had its share of parlor poker and back-room craps games, and almost every state had a lottery. All offered the same thing—money for nothing, a little buzz, an unearned life of leisure; the opportunity to flip the world the bird, with impunity. Money was a great insulator, and gambling wasn't a vice anymore; it was an industry. The Twin Cities of Sleaze, Las Vegas, and Atlantic City—the Sodom and Gomorrah of American gaming—were now being promoted as "family resort destinations." What a country!

I pulled an article on gambling's broken promises in Atlantic City and learned that the unemployment rate was basically the same as when the first casino opened. Evidence of real urban renewal was hard to find while greed and corruption flourished. All of which motivated me to find a local lead so I wouldn't have to see for myself. Just in case, I checked out the Fodor's and Mobil travel guides, and I cross-referenced a film index and put together a short list of titles on gambling and Atlantic City that I hoped to find at my local video store. At least I would *sound* like I knew what I was talking about. I was ready to roll.

First on my short list of local contacts was Ann Deaver, the missing man's teaching colleague. I called the Fox Hollow Elementary School and asked to speak with her. I knew she'd still be in class, but I only wanted to know when she left for the day, which was three-thirty. I had just enough time to recross the river and catch her on her way home.

Fox Hollow Elementary was housed in one of those early sixties Boomer buildings like the one I'd attended in Houserville near State College. I think they had about one set of suburban plans for the entire country—single-story, blond brick, with dual banks of institutional, awning-style windows; two wings running at right angles; playground out back, parking lot in front. The landscaping consisted of one towering flagpole, two stunted shrubs, and an oft-trampled flower bed. I didn't need to go inside to see the gray, vinyl-tiled floors, and pale green cinderblock walls. They were etched in my memory along with the smell of chalk dust and the sound of the dismissal bell. School days. My client told me that Ann Deaver drove an old Ford Escort. I circled the lot and found two and then settled in to wait by a battered blue baby with a PRO CHOICE bumper sticker. I sat facing the main entrance listening to some radio tunes and didn't notice the township police cruiser till it stopped beside me. The older cop in the passenger seat motioned me to roll down my window which I did.

"What can we help you with today?" the officer asked with a scowl.

"I'm waiting for my son's teacher," I said, sticking with the story I'd told the school secretary over the phone. The cop seemed unimpressed, so I added, "My son's been sick so I have to pick up his homework." Now at twenty-seven, I was old enough to have a kid in the first or second grade, but the cop wasn't buying it.

"Step out of the car, please," he said. "Let's see some ID."

I stepped slowly from the car and handed over my driver's license.

"What's this about, officer?" I asked trying to sound innocent.

The cop ignored my question and eyed me up and down like I was something left behind by an irresponsible dog walker. "Now what are you really doing here, Mr. Rotten?" he said as he handed my license to his partner.

All I could think of was how impressed my new client would be when she got wind of this little incident. I was about to retell my homework tale when a short-haired, sensibly dressed woman in her late thirties emerged from the school building and strode purposefully toward us. I took a chance and said to the cop, "Here she comes now," and then called out hopefully, "Miz Deaver."

The woman continued to her car, the blue Escort, and set down her soft, stuffed briefcase before turning to address me. "I have no idea where the weasel is these days, and I don't care what kind of trouble he's in."

"What weasel?"

"My ex-husband."

"No, no," I said, and I could tell this wasn't going over well with the cops. "I'm not looking for your ex. I'm here to see you."

"You some sort of process server?" she said. "What's with the escort?" she added, nodding toward the police cruiser.

"They're not with me," I said, trying to find a graceful way out. "Just a little miscommunication. I'm here about Billy's homework," I concluded, but got no response. "Billy Gardner's homework," I added in a pleading tone.

"Mrs. Gardner said Billy was too sick to do homework."

"He's feeling a little better, I think."

One more twist in the wind before she finally said, "It's alright, officer," and I was off the hook.

"Wait inside next time," the cop said as he handed back my ID. "All visitors need to sign in at the office."

"I'll do that," I called as the cruiser drove off and then I smiled at the schoolteacher.

"This is not a good place to talk," she said. "Follow me." And I was only too happy to comply. I'd follow a woman with attitude anywhere except the altar.

Ms. Deaver led me down to the Aspinwall Mini-Mall where I stopped for the second time that day. She pulled up outside a coffee shop called The Supreme Bean and let me buy her a cup of joe.

"Get 'em to go," she said as we stood at the counter. "They won't let me smoke in here."

And I'll bet she'd let management know just how she felt about that restriction. When I met with my client earlier in the day, it seemed she harbored mixed feelings for her husband's female friend and colleague. Now I could see why. This bossy babe could definitely inspire ambivalence. She waited outside and lit a Camel filter while I got the coffee, then we settled on a bench in front of the store.

"Security always that tight at the school?" I asked, wondering why my tie hadn't worked its charm.

"We had a first grader snatched from the school yard last week," she said.

"I'm surprised that sort of thing happens in such a nice neighborhood."

"Custody battle," she said. "Neither one of the dopes should win," she added, and I could only assume she was referring to the snatched student's parents.

I sat and watched her smoke and wondered what it would be like to be a student in her class. She may have been a bit old to inspire lust in the loins of a fourth grader, but she certainly had me intrigued. While I tried to decide how best to approach this prickly pear, she snatched the lead.

"So who hired you, Liz or Mona?" she asked.

"Who's Mona?"

"So it was Liz," she said with a smirk. "Well, you can tell sweet Lizzie that I don't have her husband. Tell her I don't *want* her husband."

"Who's Mona?" I asked again.

"Liz's mother."

"I don't think she suspects you. Ms. Gardner, that is," I said. "I think she's afraid something happened to her husband."

"Billy Boy can't handle the thought of being a father is what I think."

"They've got kids?" I asked, puzzling as I recalled the Gardners' living room and searched for toys, framed photos, any signs of mayhem. I drew a blank.

"Not yet," she said. "Liz didn't mention that she's pregnant? Shit, it's supposed to be a secret." She seemed genuinely concerned.

"Why would she keep it a secret if that's why he split?"

"Lizzie's a strange girl," she said. "Maybe she's sailing down that river in Egypt." I stared blankly. "*Dee-Nile?*" she continued. "I don't know. Maybe she didn't tell him."

"Why'd she tell you?"

"We go to the same gynecologist. I was in the office the day she found out, and I guess she couldn't control herself. She was overjoyed. Anyway, she made me promise to keep it a secret, so keep it to yourself."

"No problem," I assured her. "How long ago was this?"

"I don't know," she said and sipped her coffee. "Couple of weeks."

"You know her friend, Alison Owen?"

"A woman was with her that day in the doctor's office, but I didn't know her," she said and then paused before adding, "She was beautiful."

"Ms. Gardner?"

"Her friend," she said with a frown as she stamped out her cigarette and then reached across me to drop the butt in a trash can.

"So you've known Billy a long time?" I asked, straining to maintain my focus. The brief physical contact had caused my concentration to skip a beat.

"Since he came to Fox Hollow. Over ten years, I guess. I'd already been there a while so I helped him get settled."

"Has he been in any trouble lately? He have any problems with the principal or anything?"

"He's been slacking off a bit the past few years, but not enough to get in any trouble," she said and paused before adding, "He's missed the bus before, you know."

"My client tells me he's always come back. She's concerned he's missing school."

"He was gone two weeks once, but that was over Christmas vacation," she said. "I expect he's holed up somewhere feeling sorry for himself."

"You have any idea where that might be?"

"Billy and I were close at one time, but it's been a while," she said with a smile, before adding with an edge, "I've got cats, he developed allergies." Mature relationships are not my forte, so I fumbled with my notebook looking perplexed, before she took pity and continued, "Look, I'd like to be able to tell you that Billy Gardner was once an idealistic young teacher who became disillusioned with the system and turned sour. Truth is, he's never been in love with his work. He had potential, but he lacks commitment. He does a decent job, but his heart's not in it. He was a walk on the wild side, for Liz. Teaching's what she wanted for him, but it didn't take. Now he's playing the rebel he couldn't bring himself to be back in the day, when it mattered. He's made some poor choices in life and never had the balls to start over. No mystery."

"Just a mid-life crisis, then? Living out a Talking Heads tune?"

"Call it what you like," she said with a weary shrug. "Our generation was born old. Always feeling responsible for everything."

"Something must have gotten to him," I said. "What if he snapped? Where would he go?"

"I don't know who his friends are these days," she said, "But you may be making too much of this. On his way home, he sometimes stops at a go-go bar on Tremont. I've heard him mention 'Big Red.'"

"Seriously?"

"Unfortunately, yes," she said as she rose to go. She finished her coffee and handed me the cup.

"Wait, Big Red's the name of a bar?" I asked, confused.

"A dancer, at Boobsalot," she said, and I made a note in my book.

I thanked her for taking the time to meet with me and gave her one of my cards. "If anything comes up, you know, if you hear from Billy, or anything, just give me a call."

"Good luck," she said with a wry smile and then walked off, leaving me alone with my notes.

FOUR

Where the Boys Are

"How come I never meet women like that?" I wondered as I sat on the bench in the fading light of an autumn afternoon. Obviously, I'd just met one, but I guess I was thinking about women closer to my own age, someone I might actually have a chance with. Maybe there really was something to that experience shit, though Ann's experience with Billy had obviously not been satisfying. She had obviously *not* been his type, and for some shallow reason, I was glad.

Though I might have problems approaching the Ann Deavers of the world, I knew how to get next to Billy's type—at least, in a literal sense—and I got a big kick out of flipping to a fresh page in my notebook and writing the words "Big Red" on the top line. I now had a major motive for the reluctant dad's disappearing act, *and* the growing feeling that if I stalled my client into the weekend, Mister Missing would return to the roost on his own. I couldn't imagine he'd skip more than a week of school. All this and a field trip to Boobsalot. Things were looking up.

Before leaving the mini-mall, I stopped again at Cheswick Travel, but still no Phil. Or, as the guardian of the gate put it, "Ya just missed him." She was filing her nails this time, like a bad joke from some B-movie she'd never even seen. Again, I bit my lip—I had boobs on my mind. I'd already worked a full day, for me, but I resolved to forge ahead and pursue one last lead before packing it in.

I hadn't been to Boobsalot before, not since they changed the name from Delilah's Den, and I think it had been Thee Doll House before that. Not exactly a stable business to be in, but one that wouldn't go away. I always felt a little embarrassed about patronizing one of these fleshpots, so I mostly didn't think about it. It had been easier with a bunch of guys from my college days, but I didn't see much of the old gang anymore. I guess this was something you were supposed to grow out of, like scratching yourself and getting shit-faced. Maybe it had something to do with getting married and imagining your wife or daughter on the runway. Whatever. Today, however, was a day to let analysis rest, for I had a guilt-free ticket on the Hooterville Express. The ladies weren't the only ones working.

The lot was only half full when I arrived, but it was still early, and only construction workers had finished for the day. I fumbled my way to a seat at the bar and let my eyes adjust to the dim light.

"What'll it be?" asked the leggy barmaid wearing sprayed-on denim shorts with no visible panty line. She must have bought them two sizes too small and then washed them in hot water, but they had the desired effect. They were making me thirsty.

"Iron City," I said, grinning ear to ear. Iron City was not my normal brew, but this was definitely not craft beer country, and I wanted to fit in.

The barmaid returned quickly with my draught and picked up the twenty I had placed on the bar. As she crossed to the cash register, I couldn't help noticing her butt cheeks peeking out of her Daisy Dukes and wondered how long it had taken her to perfect that look. Not that it mattered. It was a good look. But as much as I was enjoying the view, I had to remind myself that I was working, so by the time she returned with my change, I had managed to wipe most of the grin off my face.

"When is Big Red due on?" I asked as I pushed a buck across the bar. I had arrived between dancers, so it was possible to be heard.

"Sorry, hon," she said as the bill disappeared into the scoop neck of her tank top. "Red called in sick today, but we have lots of lovely ladies coming up." And as if on cue, the next slinky sex object emerged from the dressing room to confirm her assertion.

Mid-tempo music began to pulse, and a young woman wearing spike heels, sequined G-string, and the briefest of bikini tops pranced onto the runway. My disappointment at missing Big Red was fading fast, and since I had already paid for my beer, I decided to stick around and gather some background material. Or so I told myself.

Once my eyes adjusted, I scanned the room and was struck by the obvious—the barmaid and the dancer were the only women in attendance. Oh, well, nothing unusual about that. Just a bunch of guys sitting around, politely sipping drinks, discussing the day's events. Very civilized. Yeah, right, and the Great Books Club was meeting in the back room. Most of these clowns couldn't make it through a mildly challenging magazine article. There was no shading the reality of the situation, no matter how far down you turned the dimmer switch—we were a bunch of slack-jawed slobs sitting around sucking on draughts while watching nearly naked women dance in the near dark. It took about two seconds for me to decide I could live with that.

The first performer was rhythmically challenged, and a little light in the chest area, but she had a sweet smile and a fetching way of tossing her long, dark hair, and, of course, virtually no clothes on. Or did I mention that already? She sashayed her way through two featureless tunes and then bounced into the VIP area, where patrons sat at low tables, and started hustling her tips. The seat level put the VIP's eyes on a line with the dancer's belly button. But to make herself heard above the music, the dancer had to bend over, thus swinging her tits into one guy's face while brushing her butt against the next guy's ear. An accident of engineering, to be sure, but a happy one for the hard-working dancer whose bra strap soon sprouted dollar bills.

Each performer was given a two-song head start before the next dancer began her routine. Pretty soon, my head was spinning, my drink had been freshened, and I was assessing the virtues of another curvaceous cutie. What a way to make a living! For me. Truth to tell, I had forgotten all about the missing schoolteacher whose snapshot sat in my jacket pocket. So focused was I on the flesh in front of my face that I forgot about the first dancer until she hooked her spike heel on the bottom rung of my bar stool and nudged her knee against my hip.

"Did you like my dancing?" she asked with a hint of an accent and a flash of her sweet smile.

"Oh, very much," I said as the goofy grin returned to my face. The young dancer stood close with her shoulders back and chest forward.

I reached to the bar for a bill, and she pulled out her bra strap which exposed even more of her breast. Then she snapped the strap back on the bill and asked, "Would you like a table dance?"

"Not just now. Maybe later," I heard myself saying as I flashed on the fact that I would be seeing Trudy later. I quickly groped for my missing man's photograph. "You ever seen this guy before?" I asked before the dancer had unhooked her heel.

Her smile faded some, and she looked furtively over my shoulder. "If you don't want a table dance, I have to keep moving," she said.

"How much?"

"Twenty bucks for four minutes," she replied, all business, and I nodded my assent.

Ah, the table exercise, a signature event of the Obscene Olympics—along with the inverted pole slide, the bar-top tip split, and the pelvic thrust. The dancer led me to a raised, railinged area off to one side. Privacy in plain sight. She sat me at a low table, collected my twenty bucks, and, without preamble, began rotating her hips in time to the music, swinging her snatch closer to my face with each rotation. She worked her way between my legs, then turned abruptly on her heels, and bent at the waist, which left her butt about two inches from my nose. She turned again, sat on the table in front of me, and rested her wrists on her knees. She ran her hands along the insides of her thighs and then up over her flat belly. She cupped her breasts, pushed them toward me, and continued up her body, piling her long hair on top of her head before letting it cascade over her shoulders.

"So, you ever see this guy before?" I said with a stammer as I again showed her the photo.

"Maybe once or twice," she said as she dropped the smile. "He's one of Red's pets."

"Big Red?" I said and she frowned. "She's not in today, right?"

"Called in sick," the dancer confirmed.

"You see her at all this week?"

"No, she calls in sick a lot," she said as she laid back on the table, raised her heels off the floor, and spread her legs wide. "Tomorrow's payday though," she continued as she sat up again. "Guys get paid on Friday. She'll be here tomorrow."

"Do you know if she ever dated this guy?" I asked as I felt my cheeks flush.

"We're not allowed to date any of the customers," she said pointedly, in case I had any ideas. "The owner's pretty strict about that. Red has her regulars, but none of them stay long if she's not dancing."

"She ever talk about going to Atlantic City?" I asked. "Do you know if she ever gambled at all?"

"I never talk to her that much, but she doesn't strike me as the gambling type. She gets a big enough payoff right here," she said as she stood up and started to swing her hips again, and then abruptly stopped. "You know, somebody got a postcard from Atlantic City, just the other day," she added. "It's up on the bulletin board in the dressing room."

For another ten bucks, she agreed to let me "borrow" the card. She trotted off to the dressing room with the cash, and I reclaimed my seat at the bar. It crossed my mind that I might not see her or my ten again, but she returned promptly and laid the card on the bar in front of me before resuming her tips tour without another word. My four minutes were up.

The card was a tacky, technicolor job from some small motel on the Jersey Shore. The message on the back was borrowed from Bruce Springsteen. "Put your makeup on, fix your hair up pretty, and meet me tonight in Atlantic City." At that moment, I was almost certain I had solved the case. I drained my draught and surrendered my seat before the next dancer could make it my way. This research was getting expensive.

FIVE

We Gotta Get You a Woman

The crisp, late afternoon air slowed me down some, but I was still convinced this case was ready to close. If Red failed to show for work tomorrow, I would present the postcard to my client and let her decide if Wayward Willie was really worth reeling in. "Give the bastard the boot," would be my advice. I mean, how could you take a guy back after he'd made a fool of you like that? Unless he was the President or something? But why should that even make a difference? An asshole's an asshole, right? Hopefully, I'd never face the same situation myself, and, naturally, my client would not be asking for my advice. Just the facts, jerkweed.

Even so, I was mighty pleased with myself and ready to strut some for Trudy, but I remembered today was one of her gym days, and she wouldn't be back till after six. So, instead, I popped a tape in the player and drove on home to Desolation Row.

For the record, I live in Southside, latest of the Steel City's happening 'hoods. Close to downtown, on the brink of gentrification. The city fell on hard times when the steel business crashed in the seventies. It had taken a while, but a few years back, the city fathers gave property owners some tax break for turning warehouses and whatnot into apartments, and the population soared. In another five years, the place would be unlivable, but for now, it was a nice mix of local bars, coffee houses, funky shops, and inexpensive walk-ups, with an occasional gallery down a side street. No brunch, no ferns, and very few fossils, except for the old Poles who'd lived there all their lives. Lots of Iron City and cabbage soup. Throw another pierogi in the microwave and play some Bobby Vinton on the jukebox. Worship the Steelers on Sunday afternoon.

Desolation Row, my home-away-from-home, was a local watering hole by day and cutting-edge music club by night. I occasionally met clients there, if I thought they could take a joke, but mostly I sat and sipped. The place was run by a former Pittsburgh policewoman named Casey Conlon. She took a bullet in the butt after twenty years on the force and accepted a lump sum disability so she could buy the bar. Said she wanted to stabilize the neighborhood and support the local music scene at the same time. A real urban pioneer. She considered rock 'n' roll to be some sort of religion, and she'd pull songs off the jukebox if the artist turned too commercial—something about tossing money changers from the temple. Too extreme for my tastes, but I learned not to mention Eric Clapton or The Eagles in her presence, and we got along fine. She even helped me with an occasional case, and she once offered to show me her scar, but I wasn't sure what she had in mind, so I declined. Don't get me wrong. She was a very attractive woman—five eight, well-rounded, peachy complexion, and natural blonde hair she generally wore in a ponytail when she was working, but she was like a big sister to me and that gave me pause. Any yet, you never know.

Casey was behind the bar when I arrived, and she seemed happy to see me. "Well, if it isn't Southside's most prominent private detective," she said as she walked my way, sporting an untucked, button-down oxford over a Tina Weymouth t-shirt. "Where you been hiding?"

"Home, alone, unfortunately," I said as I imagined for the thousandth time, reflective of my ongoing ambivalence, what her dimpled butt cheek must look like. "But I got paid today so I can afford to drink in public again."

"First one's on the house," Casey said as she set a mug of the local microbrew in front of me.

"Here's to public drunkenness," I said before sipping.

"One of your sleazeball attorneys finally come through with some cash?"

"I've got a real client for a change. Yours truly is working a missing person's case."

"Moving on up, eh, Frank?" she nodded in approval. "Sure you're ready for prime time?"

"I tell ya, between you and Trudy, I get no respect," I said, channeling my inner Rodney Dangerfield. "I'll have you know, this is not the first, and it's a no-brainer. Some middle-aged schoolteacher ran off to Atlantic City with a go-go dancer. He'll come home as soon as his money runs out."

"Who's your client?"

"The guy's wife."

"She hire you to bring him back?"

"She doesn't know about the stripper yet," I said and sipped. "She may not want him back."

Casey furrowed her brow, and I could tell some advice was coming my way. "Missing persons can get messy, Frank," she said. "Especially when people don't want to be found."

"Yeah, yeah, I know. Things are not always what they seem," I muttered, "But *this* seems like a classic case of Boomer burnout to me."

"Be careful, Frank. You're talking about my generation."

"Don't tell me you were one of those hippy-dippy types."

"I worked in law enforcement, remember? But I did develop some sympathies when I was in the service. What makes you think this guy was a hippie?"

"Bunch of stuff in his office. CD reissues, posters, pictures of him with long hair, and two tickets to Woodstock."

"People didn't always know what to do with all the freedom they had. Sometimes it was just a style and not a life. Something to do on the weekend."

I could sense a full-blown "back-in-the-day" lecture coming on, so in an effort to change the subject, I asked, "Pull any songs from the jukebox lately?" I should have known better.

"I'm a little concerned about what Dylan's doing up in Canada," she began earnestly, and then went on at length about this ad campaign for a bank in Toronto or someplace. It went something like, "Tangled up in debt? Don't think twice, it's alright, because our loan rate's a-gonna fall." I personally couldn't get too worked up over some song that was written before I was born, but I was preparing to listen politely for a while, when Casey pulled up and looked quizzically over my shoulder. "I'll be keeping my eye on him," she finished abruptly and walked to the other end of the bar.

I was wondering what I'd done to offend my hostess, when I sensed a presence behind me and half-turned on my stool.

"Sorry to intrude," said Alison Owen as my jaw dropped. "Mind if I join you?"

"No, please do," I managed at length, and she slipped onto the stool beside me. Man, I hate being surprised like that. I knew I must be blushing again, and the room wasn't dark enough to hide the fact. How the hell did she even know where I was? I barely knew.

"I'm sorry for causing a scene this morning," she said, and her knee brushed mine as she settled.

"No problem," I said. "Goes with the territory."

I snuck a sideways peek as Casey ambled back, and I decided that Alison was quite good at what she did. Which, as far as I could tell, was basically hanging around looking gorgeous. The slender beauty must have broken a boatload of hearts in her day. One of those women who rise out of the sea on a half shell, who live by a different set of rules, who never hear the word, "No".

She was maybe ten years older than me, but still a double-take vision in tweed jacket, faded jeans, and long wool scarf, with a colorful peasant bag slung from her shoulder. Silver kokopelli earrings dangled from her delicate lobes and twinkled through the strands of her tousled brunette tresses. I could get carried away, and I could also get a little annoyed, because I never knew if women like that just toss something on and look that good, or if they have to work at it. How much was she working on me right now?

Allie ordered a Campari and soda and then lit a slender imported cigarette after asking me if I minded. As if. "This whole situation has put everyone under a lot of stress," she said, blowing smoke.

"How the hell you find me?" I asked, recovering slightly.

"I spoke with your partner," she said, and I stared back blankly. "Desmond, he picked up your phone," she added. Desmond was my meddlesome roommate. I'd have a chat with him later.

"So what can I do for you, Ms. Owen?" I asked in what I hoped was a relaxed tone of voice. I wanted to let her know that beautiful women dropped in on me all the time. "Your friend's not having second thoughts, is she?"

"Please, call me Allie," she said and touched me lightly on the arm as Casey set down her drink, which I paid for. "Elizabeth doesn't know I'm here, and she'd be quite unhappy if she did," she added.

"Your secret's safe with me," I said, and I winked at her before I knew what I was doing. Smooth, sailor. "How did you and Mrs. Gardner get to know one another?" I asked.

"I'm an interior designer. I did some work for Liz and Billy, and we became friends."

"In their home?" I said, and she nodded. "Very tasteful."

"I'm not too sure Billy was impressed, but Liz seems happy with my work. I handle commercial properties as well, if you're ever interested."

"I'll keep that in mind."

"I was actually hoping for the chance to talk with you before you got too far along in your investigation."

"Well, I haven't found him just yet," I said, "But I'm all ears." And eyes, and knees waiting to brush against your thigh, and . . . well, she most assuredly had my attention.

"Elizabeth wasn't entirely forthcoming with you this morning," she said.

"I figured as much."

"She and Billy have been having problems for some time, and this isn't the first time he's pulled his little disappearing act," she said and sipped. "Lizzie's having trouble letting go, and Billy's not helping her at all. He doesn't love her anymore, but he's too lazy to go it alone. Anyway, I don't think you'll have much trouble finding the stupid slob, and I'm willing to pay you five hundred dollars if you let me talk to him first, before you take him home or contact Liz." She paused to drag on her cigarette. "There's a few things he and I need to discuss."

I believed her, sort of, and not just because she was beautiful. She seemed genuinely concerned about her friend. Even so, she wasn't being entirely forthcoming either, but who was I to be the first to tell her "No."

"Let me get this straight," I said since this sort of thing didn't happen to me every day. "You'll pay me five hundred dollars to steer this guy your way before I send him home?"

"That's right," she said. "I just want to talk to him."

"This wouldn't have anything to do with your friend's medical condition, would it?"

"This is something personal I need to work out with Billy before he sees Elizabeth again," she said, ignoring my question, which was alright by me. Let them have their little secret.

"Give me your phone number," I said with a smile I couldn't suppress. "I can't promise anything, but if the situation comes up, I'll see what I can do."

"I'd appreciate that," she said and pulled a business card from her bag. "My home number's on the back. Call any time."

I smiled and slipped the card in my pocket as she stubbed out her cigarette. "Say, these times that Billy disappeared before," I said to hold her a little longer. "He ever run off with anyone in particular, like have an affair?"

"That's one thing I don't think Liz would put up with," she said as she rose to go. "Mostly he gambles, but he's never lost a serious amount of money. Once he went to New York."

"City?"

"Upstate somewhere. Some farm in the Catskills, I think."

"How much money is serious?"

"I don't know exactly, but I know that's not what Elizabeth is concerned about. She wants him back so she can end it. She wants to move on with her life." She took a last sip of her drink and wished me luck.

"I'll be in touch," I promised as she walked out the door.

"I think I'm in love," I said to Casey as she cleared Allie's glass and cleaned her ashtray.

"With your new client?"

"Her friend."

"That was your new client's 'friend'?" she said with raised eyebrows. "The same client whose husband ran away with the go-go dancer?"

"One and the same. Alison Owen," I read from her business card. "President and owner of AO Design – *Interior Expressions.* What's that? Ferns and stuff?"

"Got something against ferns?"

"Nothing, in the forest. I just don't want them hanging in my hang out."

"Not to worry," she assured me.

"Quite a looker, eh?" I said waving the business card. "And I have her home phone number," I said with a leer.

"The woman who was just here was definitely a looker," Casey agreed. "But you're not her type, Frank."

"What, you think I'm too young?"

"Sweetheart, I'm more her type than you are," said the thoroughly amused barkeep, and she cupped her breasts for emphasis.

"No way!" I protested as I caught her drift.

"Sorry to burst your bubble, Frank," she said, unable to suppress a smile.

"How would you know? You're pulling my leg. How can you tell?"

"Let's just say I've had some experience in these matters and leave it at that."

"Yeah, well, I read an article just this Sunday on the 'sexual fluidity' of older women," I said, sinking fast.

"You're dreaming, dude," she said with a chuckle.

I suppose I was, but I was too young to stop. And maybe Casey *was* pulling my leg, or maybe Allie spent time on both coasts. *Think good thoughts, Frank,* I told myself, as I searched the jukebox for something from the seventies. I found some early Todd Rundgren—"a woman who has been around, one who knows better than to let you down"—and knocked back another dream-filled draught before walking home to see Trudy.

SIX

I Can Dream, Can't I?

I liked walking through the neighborhood in the early evening, letting my mind wander through that twilight time between commerce and recreation. It was like a little bit of autumn in every day, regardless of the season—a time of disembodied spirits. The loan offices and hardware stores were closing down; the cafes and clubs would soon be filling up. People were shedding their workaday selves and preparing to relax a little, step out some in search of a dream, or just kick back on the couch and take a deep breath. It was a hopeful time. *Something could go very right tonight*, people were telling themselves. Or at least one could float awhile in that buffer zone between awareness of workdays. People could grab a few hours for themselves before those dreams began to fade in a boozy haze, or it was time to set the alarm for the next day's boulder roll. What would we be if we couldn't fool ourselves a little?

I stopped at the video store and found a few of the titles on my research list and arrived at our front door just as Trudy was returning from the gym. Trudy and I had met in college, and, though she was quite the cutey-pie, we'd always been "just friends."

Just as well. We would have made a mess of things. Meaning, *I* would have made a mess of things, and I would have lost one of my best friends and reality checks.

Trudy had been an art major, and she was still pursuing her dream, but a girl's gotta eat, so she was quite grateful when I helped her land the gig at Provincial. Insurance isn't a bad day job, if you have something to live for after work. If not, it can be unbearable, which it was for me, so I had set out to pursue a dream of a different sort, which I was working on. Trying to figure out what my dream was, that is. Trying to decide what I wanted to be when I grew up. What do they call that process? Maturity, maybe? If so, I had a long way to go.

Our building was one in a row of townhomes, all owned by Rodolfo, which had been converted to apartments. Rodolfo had acquired his property the old-fashioned way; he'd inherited it. Some anonymous headbanger inhabited the first floor, Trudy and her deranged cat, Mephisto, lived on the second, while Des Holloway and I shared the third floor and abbreviated attic.

"Yo, Trude, looking good," I said as I held the outside door for her.

"Thank you, sir," she said with a smile that faded fast. "God, you reek," she added as she stepped past me.

"Hard day at the office, dear," I said as I followed her up the stairs and sniffed at my smokey clothes. "It's all your fault. You were at the gym, so I stopped off at The Row on my way home."

"Like you need an excuse to stop at The Row."

"Had to consult with Casey about my case," I said as we reached the landing and Trudy unlocked her door.

"You can only come in for a minute, Frank," she said as she entered her apartment. "I have to get ready."

"Ready for what?" I asked, stepping in cautiously. Her cat was prone to attack.

"Got a date."

"A live one?"

"Checked his pulse before I said, 'Yes.'"

"Who is he?"

"No one you'd know, and don't peek," she said, although it was only a coincidence that I frequently took out my trash just as her squires were arriving.

"I won't, if you promise to tell all tomorrow."

"Get a life, Frank," she said to me, and then cooed, "Hello, baby," to the high-strung black cat who was rubbing against her legs.

Trudy opened a cupboard for a box of kibble. The cat hissed at me and then turned its attention to its food, if that's what you can call kibble.

"I think 'Phisto needs a friend. He's a little short on social skills."

"I'll send him up after dinner, and you can read him Emily Post," she said and I flashed her a sour smile.

"So what'd you find out for me today?"

"Give me a minute to get out of my gym things," she said and slipped behind the standing screens which bisected her big room. Trudy's space was very much the struggling artist's studio—very early-Fifties Left Bank. After graduating with her Fine Arts degree, she had spent a summer in Prague. She had minored in business, but she had yet to relinquish her dream of making it in the art world. She didn't need to make it *big*; she just wanted to sell a painting before she died, and selling to friends didn't count. Anyway, she had her easel set up in one corner, and the kitchen area occupied another. The standing screens, which I helped haul home from a secondhand store, sectioned off a sleeping and dressing area. A bare bulb at the end of a wire provided illumination. I always felt like I'd walked into an atmospheric, black-and-white movie, like I should be growing a goatee or wearing a beret. Cool, man, cool. I can dig it.

The apartment did have one outstanding feature—a window facing the rear from which you could see into Rodolfo's grand, ground-level studio, where he created his "art." He was always running on about getting down to the bare essence of things, which was supposed to explain why he only worked with nude models. Rumor had it that he recorded all his "work" sessions and occasionally played the tapes at his parties, though I'd never seen one. Kinda creepy when you think of it, though. Even for me.

I heard a rustle and turned from the window just as Trudy emerged from behind a screen. She had replaced her damp, black sweatshirt with a dry one.

"So what's the scoop, Watson?" I asked.

"The only thing I did so far was the DMV check," she said, eyeing me suspiciously. "Mister had a DUI conviction about two years ago, and your client got a speeding ticket last month. No big deal. Neither one has any kind of criminal record."

I nodded thoughtfully and the cat meowed. Trudy turned to fuss with Mephisto, and I snuck another peek out the window, but I got nailed.

"Pull your head in here, pervert. Or this briefing is over."

"What? I was just checking to see if any leaves have fallen yet."

"I know what you were checking, asshole, but you need to pay attention. You're on the edge of high society here," she said with a hint of concern in her voice. "These people have been playing their games a lot longer than you've been snooping."

"What people?"

"Your client, bozo. And her family."

"My client lives in the 'burbs. Nice neighborhood, but hardly high society."

"Your client's mother is Ramona Baldwin Taft," she said, but I was drawing a blank. "Society matron? Philanthropist? Financial barracuda? Don't you ever read the gossip columns?"

"Hey, I think I heard of her," I said, remembering Ann Deaver's comment over coffee. "Someone thought she might have hired me. How'd you find out about her?"

"I worked in a bank for a while before I started at Provincial. Remember?"

"Yeah, right," I replied vaguely. "See, I told you my client could afford me."

"So what's her story?"

"Nice looking housewife, older than us. Got a girlfriend on the side," I said and winked. Trudy frowned and I continued. "She just found out she's pregnant. Apparently, the husband couldn't handle the news and ran off to Atlantic City with some exotic dancer." I paused before adding, "Everyone expects him home this weekend."

"If she expects him home, why did she hire you?" she asked, but when I opened my mouth to reply, she cut me off with a stern look and repeated her lecture. "No fooling around this time, Frank. No slacking off, or no more help from me. Now, get out. I have to get ready."

"You'll have the rest of that stuff tomorrow?" I asked as she pushed me and my bag of videos toward the door.

"Yeah, yeah. I'll give you a call from work."

"Hey, Trude," I said, stepping into the hall. "You be careful tonight." She made a face and closed the door.

I know I must have sounded condescending at times, but dating can be dangerous, and I worried about the girl. I suppose I should have worried more about myself since I hadn't even been out on a date in six weeks. Yes, six freaking weeks. But advice is one of those things that's more fun to give than receive, and since I hadn't been having much fun lately, I indulged myself at Trudy's expense. As I turned from her door and started the climb to my apartment, I heard voices. It sounded like someone was having some "fun" with my roommate.

"Why you put up with that shit?" asked an irritated woman. "I'd dump his sorry butt," was her advice.

"Oh, shut your mouth, woman," said Des in exasperation.

Des and I had been roommates in college, and we were finding it a hard habit to break, although we *were* starting to wear on each other a little. Des led a fairly active social life, but he sometimes got careless with logistics, and I sometimes got caught in the crossfire. I'd been called on before to mediate disputes, but tonight I was not in the mood. I stepped lightly into the apartment, hoping to sneak up to my room and avoid playing peacekeeper, but I barely got the door closed before the agitated female voice sounded again.

"You two-timing sack of shit!" the woman raged, except the word "shit," had been beeped out, and it was only then that I realized Des was watching TV. My long, lanky, oblivious roommate slouched alone on the couch, absently eating dry Fruit Loops straight from the box.

"You tell the bitch," he said to the screen.

I walked across the room and stood behind him. A large, tattooed woman filled the screen, eager to explain why she was willing to share her mate with the tramp who lived down the street. "I thought 'Jenny Jones' came on in the morning," I said, momentarily entranced.

"I taped it," replied Des, losing a few Loops.

"Hey, what's with this partner crap?" I said, snapping out of Jenny's spell and poking my roommate's shoulder.

"Say what?" said Des, still engrossed in the Great Debate.

I found the remote and stopped the tape which brought the national news to the screen. Des turned the sound down, reluctantly conceding that he did not live alone.

"Now, what's this 'partner' crap?" I repeated.

"What's your problem?"

"Why'd you tell that woman where to find me? The one who called earlier today."

"Oh, her," said Des. "That voice, man. It was hypnotic. I figured if she looked half as sweet as she sounded, you'd want to see her for yourself. Besides, you're always blowing people off."

"She was *quite* a dish," I said and smiled as I remembered before switching gears, "But she could've been a whacko. And blowing people off is part of my job."

"Hey, in case you hadn't noticed, I don't work for you. Some lame-ass job, poking around in other people's business," said Des who toiled part-time at The Row. "Why don't you get a real job?"

"What're you, my guidance counselor?" I said, then in a more amiable tone. "Hey, what're you doing later. I've got some videos, there's beer in the fridge, and the pizza's on me. I got paid today."

"Gotta work."

"You playing tonight?" I asked. Des played bass in some fusion group. Every other week they were fusing something else.

"Doing sound. Why don't you stop by the club?"

"I was just there," I said and shrugged. "Who's playing?"

"Tollbooth School."

"*Bor-ing*," I said. Their lead singer was a real knock-out, but they played everything at junkie speed, slow enough to sleep standing up.

"Beats sitting around here," said Des. "Meet some people. Socialize."

"I'm working a missing person's case. I need to do some research."

"You need a life, dude," he said as he turned back to Jenny Jones.

This from a man who sent fan mail to Geraldo. Whose highest phrase of praise was, "He knows he's full of shit." Who didn't own a matched pair of socks, and whose loftiest career ambition was to launch a local cable version of America's Most Humiliating Home Videos. "It could fly, dude," he'd tell me. "This burg eats that shit up." He may have been right, but he'd have to move off the couch to prove it, and that was not about to happen. But Des did pay half the rent and kept his mess confined to his room. And even though he wasn't exactly an engaging conversationalist, he did work most nights, and he was gone by the time I got out of the shower.

I slipped into some lounge wear—jeans and a flannel shirt—and then sat at my desk and sifted through my mail, most of which Des had already opened. Another of his endearing habits. If I left anything unopened on my desk for longer than three days, Des considered it fair game. All of the current crop was junk, though, and I consigned it to the recycling bin. I hit the "Play" button on my answering machine and found messages from my newest client, who already wanted an update; from an attorney's office, requesting that I stop by to discuss a scene investigation; and finally, from Alison Owen, complete with my "partner's" smooth-talking interruption.

I made a note to stop by the attorney's office and then wandered into the kitchen area in search of some grub. I found a frozen tub of vegetable lasagna which I popped in the microwave. This was as close to cooking as Des or I ever came, except for pasta and the odd omelet, although we did intend to buy a toaster. I poured myself half a jelly glass of jug red and sat on the couch for some channel surfing. Three clicks in, I was stopped by the unmistakable strains of an old detective show theme, and I paused to spend a few moments with my mentor. Sitting on the sofa, sipping wine, I remembered my last day at The Provincial Insurance Company of America. Getting fired came as a complete surprise, though it shouldn't have. I had been warned. Repeatedly.

It's a weird experience, being let go. They have an Orwellian Termination Script which they follow to the letter. Very careful, these provincials. First thing in the morning your supervisor invites you into the manager's office, which is never a good sign. The manager recites your Sins Against the Enterprise and suggests it's time to move on. If you do the right thing and resign, you're given a severance package to soften the blow. But if you make a fuss and force them to fire you, well, then they get nasty. No severance, no nuthin'. Just your self-respect, if you have any left, and the lingering fear that the lumbering behemoth will find some way to exact its revenge. Because the whole mess is your fault for ever coming to work there in the first place.

Anyway, I shed my self-respect and opted for the severance package. Security escorted me to a conference room where a Human Resources ghoul waited to explain the terms of my release. I signed off in shock, absolving the company of any blame. A guard watched while I rummaged through my desk, ostensibly packing up personal belongings, but the only thing I took was a postcard from Bogg Island sent by a former flame. I was out the door by mid-morning. No future for you, Frank. The career is dead, long live the career! But what career? You mean I actually have to decide what to do with my life; it won't just happen? I drove around in a rage for an hour thinking of all the smartass things I should have said to Manager Newspeak before I gave it up. Then, still following the script, I started feeling enormously sorry for myself. What to do, what to do, what to do?

At length, I picked up a six-pack of Iron City, drove home, and crashed on the couch. A & E was in the midst of a Rockford Files marathon, and I sat through six episodes straight, or until my beer ran out. I can't remember which. Anyway, I had a religious experience, of sorts. Not quite Saul-on-the-Road-to-Damascus, but an epiphany, at least. Essentially, I saw the light. I knew what I wanted to be, and I didn't have to grow up. Next day, I applied for unemployment, bought an answering machine, and went into business for myself. Frank Rotten, Discreet Investigations— semi-retirement at an early age. I had to admit that *The Rockford Files* was way past its expiration date, but Old Jimbo taught me everything I needed to know about the detective business—style is essential, but it doesn't have to be flashy to be effective; dodge the line of fire, *and* responsibility; finally, let your lowlife friends do all the dirty work. Oh, and maintain contact with as many sleazeball attorneys as you can stand. Over time, I got business cards, an ad in the Yellow Pages, a separate phone line, and even an official license. Top of the world, ma!

The microwave beeper pierced my reverie, and I went to retrieve my lasagna. I sat at the coffee table and scarfed my pasta pie while Jim solved his case. The pool cleaner did it, whatever *it* was, and Jim got the girl, at least for dinner. What a guy! I wondered briefly what Alison Owen had done for dinner and then decided to clean up some rather than torture myself.

I heard a nervous fuss in the hall downstairs when Trudy's date arrived, but I resisted the urge to peek. See how mature I can be? After that I had the place to myself, but I wasn't in the mood for introspection. I had a *life*; it just wasn't interesting enough to bear much scrutiny at the moment. And you couldn't see into Rodolfo's studio from our window, so I brewed a pot of coffee and settled in to do some research, such as it was.

First up, *Atlantic City*, which I remembered right away I had seen before, but I still watched long enough to catch Susan Sarandon's lemon juice lavabo. Tang! Next, I tried *California Split*, but Robert Altman's simul-talking soundtrack drove me crazy. Say what? Finally, I gave *The Gambler* a shot, even though I'm not a big James Caan fan, but after *The Godfather*, I couldn't see him as a college professor. I was beginning to get the point though. Gambling is compulsive. People get addicted to the boost, the juice, the thrill of living on the edge, at least while they're laying a bet. Maybe it *was* a disease, but it didn't seem to be contagious. Maybe everybody has a weakness. You just need to figure out what it is and steer clear. I don't know. I drifted off before the end, despite the coffee, wondering what my weakness was, and inviting dreams of older women.

SEVEN

Good Morning, Mister Rotten

The next morning started way too early when the phone on the table at the head of the couch, where I slept all night, rang obscenely at seven-thirty. Someone must have dropped a hat; Trudy was in love again.

"He's dreamy," Trudy enthused in her phone voice, calling from work. "He's got a pierced ear, a steady income, and he does *not*, repeat, *does not* live with his mother."

"Uh-huh," I mumbled, waiting in vain for my head to clear.

"His mother's dead, Frank. Isn't that wonderful?" The poor girl's last romance had been sabotaged by a Meddling Mom. She was seriously into orphans now.

"That's great, Trude," I said and yawned. "What time is it?"

"You don't sound happy for me, Frank."

"You woke me up."

"You said you wanted to hear all about it."

"And I do," I assured her. "How 'bout I meet you for lunch?" Trudy worked seven-thirty to three-thirty so lunch came early.

She was disappointed she didn't get to tell her story right away, but we made a date for eleven.

I sat on the couch trying to retrace the steps which had led to me sleeping alone in the middle of the living room. I spied the stack of videos and noticed that I'd left one in the machine, and it started coming back to me. Remote control made it too easy to just stay where you were, and Des apparently hadn't made it home to tuck me in. I was debating whether it was worth the effort to crawl up to my bed or crash again on the couch when a knock came at the door. You can't reach our door without being buzzed in from the street so I thought it must be the head banger from the first floor, whom I decided to ignore, until the knock came again with greater insistence.

"Alright already," I mumbled as I stumbled across the room. Then, displaying an acute lack of judgment, I opened the door to a thick-necked goon suited up like a chauffeur—a yard-wide, walking, talking warning on the dangers of steroid abuse.

"Someone wants to see you," he said with a blank expression. I moved to close the door, but the goon had fast feet. The door bounced back at me. "Downstairs," he added.

Who was I to argue? Besides, I could use a little air, maybe pick up the morning paper and a cup of joe. I started down the stairs ahead of my escort, shuffling and slouching, trying to look cool, but I couldn't shake the thought of those bone breakers from *The Gambler*. James Caan was having the last laugh, big time, and yet I couldn't think of anyone I had pissed off to that extreme. I can be an asshole at times, but I've never been one to inspire intense emotions, just annoyance. In any case, the

Lou-Ferrigno-look-alike filled the stairwell behind me so there was no turning back, and the first floor headbanger wouldn't be of much help even if he were at home. I resolved to look cool as long as possible and then make a break at the last minute, but when I pushed through the door to the street, I found the sidewalk early-morning empty. Nothing more sinister than trash swirled. I blinked about in my slept-in stocking feet until faux-Ferrigno's firm hand guided me to an incongruously impressive, pearl gray Rolls Royce Phantom which sat idling at the curb.

Ersatz Lou opened the car door, and I settled into the ample rear seat opposite a way older woman who'd obviously had a tuck or two. She wore nylon breeches and a tweed jacket with suede patches on the elbows. A hard-shell riding helmet lay on the seat between us, and she idly slapped a horse crop against her knee-high leather boots. Quite the first impression.

"Good morning, Mister Rotten," she said with a growl. "Would you care for some coffee?" One of those fancy thermal pots sat on an elaborate tray which folded out of the seat back.

"Black," I replied.

"My name is Ramona Baldwin Taft," she said as she poured. "You've been hired by my daughter to find her worthless husband, William."

"What's it to you?" was the best I could manage as I sipped the strong brew.

"I would also like to locate Mister Gardner," she said, ignoring my attitude. "And I have every confidence in your ability to do so."

"Your daughter got my name out of the Yellow Pages. Where's the confidence coming from?"

"My son-in-law is not very bright. He won't be hard to find. He'll run out of money and do something stupid."

"Why not just wait for him to come home?" I said as I gazed around at the rich interior. I closed my eyes and inhaled—strong coffee, soft leather, stale cigarettes, and dubious intentions.

"I don't want him *home*," she said as she slapped her boot. I had to wonder why she wanted rid of her grandchild's sire, but what did I know about rich people? "You see, I never liked the boy," she continued, answering my unasked question. "Not that he wasn't attractive enough in his youth, but I never thought he'd amount to much, and he hasn't." She paused. I sipped and scanned for doughnuts.

"William is obviously unhappy," she resumed, "But he knows he'll get nothing if he initiates divorce proceedings, and Elizabeth refuses to take action herself. She's still young enough to start over, but she needs to start soon. Find that poor excuse for a spouse, tell him I've raised my offer to a quarter of a million dollars. He'll know what he needs to do to collect. I'll pay you one thousand to make the offer, and five thousand if he accepts."

"You're talking dollars, right?"

"Of course, dear boy. In cash if you prefer."

"Your daughter know you're here?" I asked, wondering at the same time if I could manage to collect from both Allie *and* Mona, and flashing to the time in college when I used the same paper in two different classes and got a "B" in both.

"There is no need for her to know. This is between you and me."

"So, you just want me to deliver your message to Worthless Willie, and keep my mouth shut?"

"That's essentially it," she said and paused before continuing. "I pride myself on my appreciation of the ethically challenged, but perhaps I've misread you, Mister Rotten. If you have a problem with the arrangement, please let me know now."

"No, I don't see any real conflict."

"I didn't think you would," she said, and I had the vague impression I'd just been insulted, but I didn't waste much time worrying about it. I was too busy thinking what I'd do with the bonus. I took a last swig of my coffee and set the cup on the tray.

"I'll be in touch," she promised and then off to the hunt she was, leaving me on the sidewalk in my socks.

I waved as the Rolls rounded the corner and then turned back to the spot it had occupied at the curb. Already I was beginning to doubt what had just happened, so I jogged to the end of the block for a last look, but the great car was gone.

"Hey, man," a voice called behind me. It was Des returning from who knew where. "What's up, dude?" he asked as I stumbled toward the stoop.

"Did you see that?"

"You lock yourself out?"

I stopped and slapped my pockets and realized that I had, indeed, locked myself out of the building. "Shit," I said.

"Hey, was that a Rolls I saw you getting out of?"

"Yeah, man, it was," I said, delighted I hadn't dreamed it. "Can you believe it? High society taking me for a test drive."

"Dressed like that? No wonder you got dumped on the curb."

It was too much to explain that early in the morning, so I didn't even try. "Where've you been all night?" I asked as Des opened the outside door. I stopped and inspected the lock but could find no sign of tampering, as if I knew what to look for.

"Yolanda came by the club, and we partied with the band some," Des said over his shoulder as he climbed the stairs. "But things got out of control so I just crashed at her place."

"Crashed at her place, huh?" Yolanda was a looker, and I happened to know that Des had a thing for her.

"It's not how you think, man."

"How is it, Des? It's been so long for me I can't remember."

"Get a life," advised Des, yet again, as he entered our apartment. "And put some clothes on next time you go out." He looked down at my feet. "Hey, are those my socks?" he asked, but I ignored the question and pushed past him through the door. They *were* his socks.

"Hey, you ever been to Atlantic City?" I asked to change the subject. "I may be headed that way."

"I've seen the movie. Who's that Thelma-and-Louise chick who did the bit with the lemon? They got some big-ass elephant on the beach."

"That was Susan Sarandon, and that elephant is actually out of town a ways." My research was paying off.

"Never been, man," said Des, pouring a cup of old, cold coffee and placing it in the microwave. "I'm not a gambler. I only play sure things." This from a man whose band hadn't played a gig in weeks. "When you going?"

"I don't know. Maybe this weekend. My missing man disappeared down there."

"You'll be missing a killer party, dude. Hey, you ever pay the rent?" he asked anxiously and I nodded. Relieved, he added, "I hear Rodolfo's got some new tapes."

"Has anyone ever seen one of those tapes?"

"I know some chick who was *in* one," said Des. "Threatened to sue his ass if he didn't help her get into art school."

"Sounds like a winner, alright, but I may have to pass. And you'd better not mention those tapes to Trudy. She'd go nuts."

"Hey, if you do go to AC, let me know," said Des, sidestepping the tape issue. "I'll give you five bucks to play on black twenty-seven."

"A sure thing, right?"

Des ignored me and headed for the shower. He had an early rehearsal with the band. I forget what they were fusing that week. I climbed to my room and stretched out on my bed while visions of camcorders danced in my head. If the crop-wielding Queen Mother's offer was legit, I could be close to stepping up a level. And, if I could convince the absent educator to run away a rich man, then I'd have a down payment on my surveillance van. The world was full of fatherless children, what was one more?

Lying there in the semi-dark, I started wondering how my own life might have been different if I'd never known my father. I mean, assuming we had enough money and all to get along. Could I really be any more screwed up? My father had left before I turned five and I hadn't seen him much since. How much had his intentional absence affected me? Did I really need another person disapproving of what I was doing with my life, or was one enough? Besides, he'd started a new family in Chicago, so how much of a father did I still have?

This line of thought was making me cranky. I was sorry I'd started, and glad to remember the message from attorney Karen Stanley requesting a scene investigation. I had just enough time to shave and stop in on my favorite ambulance chaser before meeting Trudy for lunch.

EIGHT

Can I Get a Witness?

Karen Stanley was a bottom feeder and proud of it. She made her reputation on local cable with a series of sleazy ads aimed at chronically unemployed couch potatoes who imagined they'd been injured in an accident. The ads starred Karen in a short skirt sitting on an old oak desk showing a lot of leg. She liked to tell people that the desk had been her father's and that he'd given it to her when she graduated. I happened to know she bought it herself at an estate sale, but I had nothing against a little revisionist history. I reworked my own resume every day.

"I need a scene sketch and a few pictures of the car," Karen was saying across the same desk that had been featured in the ads. Unfortunately, she was sitting behind it, not on it. "Oh, and I need a witness."

"That intersection's out in the middle of nowhere," I said scanning a county map. "Nobody saw this happen."

"I'd have a much better case if somebody did," she said suggestively. Now she may have been asking me to do

58

something—something not-quite-kosher, yet worth a tidy bonus—but knowing Karen, I'd never get her to say so. Dance on, McDuff.

"I probably won't get out there till Monday."

"No problem. I haven't even taken this guy's statement yet." We were waiting in Karen's office to do just that, but the guy was late, and Karen was not likely to wait much longer. "You pretty busy, Frank?" she asked, to make conversation.

"I'm working a missing person's case right now, but otherwise it's been slow."

"What have you got, another teenaged runaway?"

"A grown-up, of sorts. Unhappy husband, reluctant father." I could tell by her expression that my guy was not her type. She glanced at her watch, and I knew I was almost out of there, so I made a pitch for some background info on my case. "Say, you do divorce work, don't you?"

"Some," she said, shifting warily in her seat. "It's good money, but not my cup of tea. Things can get real ugly."

"I'll bet," I said and continued with my pitch. "Supposing this guy of fairly modest means, a schoolteacher, say, is married to this woman who is due to inherit a ton of money; she may already have inherited a ton of money. If they got divorced, would he be entitled to any of that?"

"Not necessarily, depends on whether they had a prenup," she said. "Even without one, inheritances are not generally considered to be community property." I frowned. "This wouldn't have anything to do with your case, would it?"

"I don't know," I said, and I really didn't.

"Any aspect of a divorce can be contested," said the star of all those cable commercials. "If your missing man needs an attorney, Frank, have him give me a call."

"I have to find him first, but let me take one of your cards." I plucked one from the stylish holder on her desk.

"Doesn't look like my guy's going to show, and I've got other clients waiting," Karen said with another glance at her watch. "Paying clients."

"Hey, we'll have to do dinner some time," I said as I moved to the door. I wasn't in her league for a long-term relationship, but she did give me a call every once in a while, when she got lonely. I could handle being used like that.

"A girl's gotta eat," she said, and I started to think that I really did have a life. Or could have if I only applied myself.

I made small talk with a few of the paralegals who usually set up the scene investigations and then decided to walk the five blocks to my lunch date with Trudy. It was a nice enough day by Pittsburgh's standards—the temperature was above freezing and nothing was falling from the sky—but I didn't take much note of it at the time. I always felt a little weird walking to meet Trudy at work. Something in the air around that office building raised my anxiety level. The theme from *The Twilight Zone*—doo-doo, doo-doo, doo-doo, doo-doo—sounded like some truck-warning, backing beeper. I felt a lingering trepidation that I could get sucked back in, like a lapsed Catholic returning to the faith, and yet I liked the idea of testing myself. I remembered a story I'd heard in school about Gandhi after he declared celibacy.

Supposedly, old Mohandas slept in the same bed with a beautiful, willing woman on occasion to steel his resolve. And legend
has it, he always met the test. Yeah, right. More like, "rose to the
occasion." Whatever you say, Mahatma. Not that working for
Provincial had been that awful, or that they'd ever hire me back,
but it had been such a sneaky, seductive experience. I graduated
from Allegheny State with little idea about what I wanted to
do, and Provincial needed claim reps. Whoever thinks about
going into the insurance business? I thought I'd hang in just long
enough to get my head straight and my butt settled in a nice pad,
and then I'd meet a girl and move on to what was real. Three
years later, I looked up at my desk divider and saw my name
on that professional, plastic plate, and I felt like I was fading
away. Cold Shower City. Letting the days go by. I guess I started
mouthing off a bit after that, making inappropriate suggestions
and whatnot, until Provincial made *their* suggestion that I'd
be happier elsewhere. I didn't argue. I didn't have a clue as to
what I would do, but I didn't argue. It was alright for someone
like Trudy who had her easel to hang onto, but someone like
me could get lost and wake up after twenty years in the middle
of that Talking Heads' tune. ("And you may ask yourself . . .")
Or I could wake up in a cardboard box on the street somewhere
and wonder why I'd thrown it all away. Unfortunately, only time
would tell.

Trudy was already waiting when I arrived at our prearranged
street corner. She insisted I was late, but I think she'd left her desk
early after a particularly aggravating phone exchange. Cranky
callers—the bane of the profession. No one was ever at fault in
an auto accident, not if you listened to the people involved. ("He

should've seen me coming." "She stopped short right in front of me.") I listened to her wind down for ten minutes as we ordered deli sandwiches and found a bench in the art park across the street. Trudy was nervous about eavesdroppers so we ate alfresco whenever we could.

"I fixed that asshole," she said still fuming. "I only wish I could be there when he gets his next renewal. They'll jack up his premium good after reading my report."

"Steady, girl. I thought you were going to tell me about your date last night."

"I thought you didn't want to hear about it."

"Geez, give me a break, I was sleeping."

She took a bite of her tuna on wheat toast and pretended to ignore me for a minute, before finally saying, "He seemed very nice, but I don't want to jinx it." And I had to respect her suspicion of feeling too good about something to talk about it.

"Alright, what have you got on my missing man?" I asked, and then I remembered the Rolls. "Hey, did I tell you I met the mother-in-law?"

"You never tell me the good stuff."

"Right after I talked to you this morning, this goon appears at my door and drags me down to this pearl-gray Rolls Royce to meet none other than Ramona 'Big Bucks' Baldwin Taft. We had coffee in the back of her car," I said, still impressed.

"What did she want?" asked Trudy, a little irritated at being upstaged.

"She wants to get rid of her son-in-law, and she wants me to help," I said excitedly, but Trudy only frowned. "I don't know exactly what's going on, but she's planning to offer the guy big bucks to initiate divorce proceedings because her daughter won't do it on her own. Maybe she doesn't want him to have anything to do with the kid."

"Isn't that a conflict of interest?"

"I don't see how," I said, trying not to think about it too much, because obviously it was. "I'll still find the guy. I'll just make more money for doing it."

"He certainly doesn't sound like much of a father figure," said Trudy, still sulking about the lack of attention, but long past the point where she'd take exception to my ethical equivocations.

"So, what did you dig up?" I asked. She took another bite of her tuna and chewed it thoroughly before launching her report.

"Your client owns the house outright, husband and wife each own a car. She has significant sums socked away in stocks and securities, real conservative stuff, looks like the remnants of a trust fund or something. There's a savings account in Elizabeth's name with a ten-thousand-dollar balance. William's has five hundred, and there's a joint checking account with about twenty-five hundred. Several joint credit cards with zero balances," she said and paused for effect, "And, ten cards in his name only maxed out at five thousand each. He pays the minimum amount due each month on each one."

"Wow! He's in some deep shit. I wonder if the missus even knows about those?"

"Probably not. He has the bills sent to a PO box."

"I'll bet Old Mona knows."

"I wouldn't be surprised. She's got money out the wazoo, and she throws her weight around."

"How do you know about her?"

"This woman is notorious in city financial circles. A real barracuda. Her father owned a steel mill back in the day. He sold out a few years before the industry crash, and diversified big time, with Mona at his side. She runs everything now."

"So, not just an idle threat."

"Watch your back," warned Trudy. "Hell, watch your front."

I promised to be careful, but the camcorders were dancing again. Ramona had read me well, and, unfortunately, my years in the insurance business had taught me that playing by the rules didn't always yield a just result. You could do the right thing and still get screwed. After lunch, I walked Trudy back to work, walked right up to the old door, and peered into the lobby, tempting fate. And then I found a phone kiosk and checked my answering machine. The only message was from my client, and I immediately regretted my promise of daily updates. I had thought about working on my scene investigation before stopping off at Boobsalot to see Big Red, but I decided instead to try Phil Cheswick again. Clients appreciated the appearance of some effort, especially if you have no concrete results to offer.

I followed the river back to Aspinwall and found the same gum-cracking greeter behind her desk, but still no Phil. I was determined to cross the travel guy off my list, so I took a seat and loudly announced my intention to wait. And I waited patiently, at first, until the canned tuneage from the unseen speakers began to grate. I decided to make a nuisance of myself and proceeded to paw through a brochure rack.

"Do you think Kathie Lee has ever really been on one of those cruises?" I inquired of the unsettled receptionist as Barry Paul Manilow McCartney tore into "Mandy on the Run."

The young woman warily rose from her desk and slipped into the glass-walled cubicle in the rear. She had a brief, animated phone conversation and then returned to her seat and announced, "Mister Cheswick will be here in just a few minutes."

I settled down with an article on the artificial islands of the Caribbean and wondered what I could do for my next act of impatience. But surprisingly enough, not twenty minutes later, a disheveled man in his early forties with curly hair and a graying mustache breezed through the holding pen and nervously acknowledged my presence.

"I'll be with you in a minute," he said as he passed.

"Sure thing," I said with a smile. My obnoxious routine had never worked this well before. Old Phil was letting his insecurity show.

The receptionist followed him into his own private Pittsburgh and I heard him say, "Who is this guy?" before the door closed behind them. But she had never bothered to ask, so several minutes later, Phil still wore his anxious frown as I was ushered into his office.

"Hi, have a seat," said Phil, squirming slightly. "Sorry to keep you waiting. I was doing some work from home today. Can I get you something to drink? Coffee? Soda?"

"I'm fine, thanks."

"Now what group did you say you were from, Mister . . ?"

"Rotten. Frank Rotten," I said, not sure how to take advantage of his anxiety. "I represent the Missing Husbands of America."

Phil paused uncertainly and then asked, "And you're interested in a tour to where?"

"Atlantic City," I said, and the furrows on his brow deepened.

"I'm not sure I understand. We haven't canceled any tours to AC," he said, half to himself. "You're not here about a deposit then?" Phil apparently owed a few refunds.

"I'm here about a missing schoolteacher named 'William Gardner,'" I said. "He took your casino excursion last weekend and never made it back." I pulled out the missing man's school snap and handed it across the desk.

"Who are you again?" he asked, scanning the photograph.

"I'm a private investigator. I was hired by this guy's wife to find out what happened to him."

"Let me get this straight," said Phil as irritation replaced anxiety. "I don't owe you any money?" I shook my head and he scowled. "And you pulled me in here to check out this loser who couldn't find his way back from the Shore?" He was relieved, but still annoyed.

"I never said anything different."

"I don't know nothing about any missing person," he said and took another quick look at the picture to be sure. "And I haven't been on one of those buses in weeks."

"My client holds you responsible."

"For what? For losing her husband? Christ almighty, I'm no babysitter. This shit happens all the time."

"What, people disappear?"

"You oughta lose the attitude, sport," he said. "This is Atlantic City we're talking about. Guys get hung over, they sleep late, they meet somebody, they miss the bus. Sooner or later, they find their way home."

"It's been a week now and nobody's heard from him."

"What's that got to do with me?"

"This kind of publicity could be bad for business."

"What publicity?" he said with a shrug. "There's people that like to gamble some and see a show. These tours sell themselves. There's no publicity."

"My client is well-connected in this town. If this gets splashed all over the evening news, how many tour groups will be looking for refunds?"

"Christ, why bust my balls?" he wanted to know, and I had no answer. I had no idea at that point what I was hoping to accomplish. "Listen, I don't even handle those tours," he continued. "Terry takes care of them. Hold on a sec. Theresa," he called loudly through the open door.

Theresa took her time. The languid receptionist lowered her nail file to the desktop, then trudged back, leaned against the door jamb, and folded her arms in front of her, cradling her ample bosom. Why hadn't I noticed before how nicely she was built?

"Terry, hon, you ever see this guy before?" Phil asked as he reached out with the photograph.

She moved to the side of the desk to take the snapshot from her boss. "I seen him on the casino trips a few times," she said, wearily studying the shot. "He's the guy who missed the bus last week."

"You remember anything unusual?" I asked. "Was he with anybody in particular?"

"He went down by himself, but I think I saw him with some blonde in the casino. Somebody said he won big playing craps. We waited about a half-hour on Sunday morning and then left without him."

"You report this to anybody?" I asked Phil.

"Report what? That some slob missed the bus?" he said and shrugged. "Who would I report it to?"

"You might have called his wife?"

"What wife? You think I know who these people are? Most of them don't *want* me to know. Some of them shouldn't be there."

"I think she called on Monday morning," said Terry. "Somebody called, wanted to know about the guy who missed the bus, wanted to know where we stayed."

"And what'd you tell her?" I asked.

"I told her just what I told you."

"You told her about the blonde?"

"Give me a break," said Terry, which I took to be a "no."

"You sure she was a blonde, not a redhead?"

"Young blonde. Looked like a pro."

"A hooker?"

"Hooker, escort, whatever," she said with a shrug. "She wasn't volunteering her time."

"How would you know?"

"Oh, puh-lease," said Terry as she rolled her eyes and handed me back the photo.

"You tell the wife where you stayed?"

"The Shifting Sands Motor Inn," she said. "I gave her the number."

"You ever been on one of my tours?" asked Phil to lighten the mood. "We got a group leaving tonight, right, Ter?"

"Midnight, from the parking lot," Terry confirmed.

"You oughta go down there and see for yourself. On me. The pros aren't hard to pick out," he added with a wink. "Add his name to the list," he said to Terry. "Now give me a break. I got work to do."

I followed Terry back to the outer office and let her add my name to the list, even though I wasn't sure yet I would be making the trip. On my way out the door, she emphasized that the bus left at twelve sharp. I could leave my car in the lot over the weekend.

I put a mental check mark next to Phil's name and stepped out into the middle of the afternoon. I had some time to kill before my return trip to Boobsalot, and I considered calling my client, but what could I tell her? That her advance was almost gone, and her husband was still missing? That her best friend and her mother had thrown their hats in the ring? That Darling Bill had last been seen in the company of a young, blond professional? I didn't think so. She'd only pressure me to travel to AC and I wasn't ready to give up on Rodolfo's party just yet. I still had that postcard to play. If I could confirm a connection between Billy and Big Red, Mrs. Gardner might decide that her husband was not worth finding and call off the dogs.

I bought a copy of the nation's newspaper and walked around to The Supreme Bean. I sat with a cup of cappuccino and an almond biscotti till passing school buses signaled the start of another rush hour.

NINE

Dance, Ballerina, Dance

Was it "rush hour" because everyone was hurrying to get somewhere, or because people got such a boost being away from work? Another of those irrelevant "chicken-or-egg" debates that seemed to occupy far too much of my time. Something for me to think about on the drive over, perhaps, but nothing to discuss with any of the horn dogs lining the Boobsalot bar on a Friday afternoon. These guys had not gathered to argue philosophical absurdities. There was nothing intellectual about their pursuit. They stood at the gateway to the weekend with money to burn and brains unplugged. Newly liberated, brimming with expectation, they were eager to wash away the bitter taste of another week wasted with work. They wanted to shoot some shit, dish some dirt, and talk some trash. Let the ladies strut their stuff. They wanted to see some skin.

The make-up of the crowd was pretty much the same as the day before, but with clusters of white collars gathered here and there. Very democratic place, Boobsalot. We're all sleazeballs under the skin. The same leggy barmaid was working the taps, and she delivered my draught with a look of recognition that didn't so much say she remembered me as she knew a sleazeball when she saw one. I swear she was wearing the same sprayed-on shorts with an even skimpier, tighter tank top that brought her nipples into high relief.

Ah, trolling for payday gratuities, a time-honored tradition in the go-go business. Get your slice before they put away the pie. The atmosphere reminded me a bit of a shopping mall at Christmastime. A bustling crowed buzzed with anticipation while management pulled out all the stops to keep the customers happy and the cash flowing. There was a chicken-wing buffet working, and they'd even hired a dee-jay to hype the crowd between dancers. He referred to himself as "your entertainment director for the evening," and he said a lot of cornball things like, "Are you ready for the weekend?" which didn't get much of a response. But he did set a brisk pace and kept the exotic parade rolling, *and* he'd apparently helped the performers put together a few routines, which was a nice touch.

He had one fresh-faced kewpie doll enter to the tune of "Good Morning Little Schoolgirl". The virginal-looking young lady wore an approximation of a Catholic girl's school uniform, which she promptly lost, and the dee-jay followed with Billy Joel's "Only the Good Die Young" ("Come out, Virginia . . ."). Another dancer, sporting a frilly half-slip, pranced to the theme from *Petticoat Junction* until the slip slipped to reveal an emerald G-string, upon which the disc-spinner segued into *Green Acres.* The place to be.

I was having a good time inflating my expense account, but I had nursed two draughts through an hour of entertainment and still no Big Red. Though Sexy Shorts assured me that Red had not called in sick again, I was ready to take the dancer's absence as confirmation of my theory that she'd run off to Atlantic City with Mister Missing. And, I had decided to offer this "proof" to my client after just one more round of surveillance, when the entertainment director announced the arrival of "what you've all been waiting for." With that dramatic introduction, the top-billed booty-shaker made her entrance to the slinky strains of Sam the Sham's "Little Red Riding Hood" ("You sure are lookin' good"), which must have been her signature tune since the crowd knew just what to expect and howled along with Sam as if on cue.

I must admit she was worth the wait, even though her presence cut the bottom out of my theory. She briefly wore a hip-length, hooded, red velvet cape which played peek-a-boo with her tight, tawny butt as she made her way through the woods to grand-ma's place. The strikingly beautiful redhead moved with an air of voluptuous athleticism which couldn't completely conceal her disdain for her audience. And yet, when the wolf made his appearance in the form of Steppenwolf's "Born to Be Wild," well, the crowd went wild. Red ripped through the classic rock tune and then abruptly exited to the groaning disappointment of the vibrating throng. The dee-jay assured us that she would be out shortly, which she was, and the nearly naked woman started working the room.

Nobody danced while Red hustled tips, but the dee-jay goosed her a bit by playing a medley of hits about money, and even dis-played a sense of irony by tossing in The Animals' "House of the Rising Sun." I was expecting a long wait through multiple lap dances, but Red arrived at my elbow before I had the chance to frame my first question. She looked older up close, and I realized she must work hard for her firmness.

"Did you like my dance?" she said with an inaccessible smile.

"I need to talk to you for a few minutes," I said, and she suggested a table dance, which I was ready for, but I wasn't prepared for the price—forty bucks for four minutes. No wonder she made her way so quickly around the room. I hesitated and she was about to move on, but I had come this far, and I couldn't imagine getting this close again, so I agreed. Luckily, I had forty bucks left in my wallet.

Red led me back to the table-dance corral, and I was dimly aware of the murmuring approval of my peers. The dee-jay played something up-tempo, and the crowd was distracted by the arrival of another dancer on the runway. I was left alone with Big Red. She may have had an attitude, but she was a pro, and she was good at what she did, which was make me feel like she was the most desirable woman alive, while making it clear there was no hope I'd ever have her. Body language can be very expressive. But the distance in her demeanor, even as she shook her tits in my face, made it easier to draw the snapshot from my pocket and ask, "You ever see this guy before?"

She seemed surprised, as if to say, "You really did want to talk with me, you little weenie," but she took the picture and peered at it in the dim light, then handed it back, and said, "Who are you?"

"A private detective. I've been hired to find this guy."

"What's that got to do with me?"

"He used to come in here," I said as I held up the picture again. "You recognize him?"

"I may have seen him at the bar a few times."

"You ever see him outside the bar?"

"I never see anyone outside the bar," she said and handed back the photo.

"You ever talk to him?"

"I may have, but I don't really remember."

"He ever talk about gambling, or running away together, or Atlantic City?"

"I don't pay much attention to what anybody says in this place, pal."

"So he didn't send you this postcard?" I asked and handed her the card.

She looked it over front and back. "This was on the bulletin board in the dressing room," she said, tapping the card against her thumbnail. "This shit happens all the time. Guys get carried away."

At this point, she was making no effort to move to the music. She stood in front of me, tall and gorgeous with slippered feet planted apart, folded arms supporting her breasts. The Hooterville Express was approaching the end of the line. The clock was running, and my smoke-thin theory was drifting away on an exhaust-fan breeze.

"Guys don't *disappear* all the time," I said. "That card was sent from the Jersey Shore. This guy left a note to his wife saying he was running away to Atlantic City, with you." I was fumbling in the dark for the right button to push. Needless to say, all I did was piss her off.

"You're full of shit," she said.

"How do you explain the card?"

"Why would I even try? I'm obviously not in Atlantic City." She looked the card over again before handing it back. "That card is not addressed to anyone in particular, and it's not even signed," she added with more than a hint of her trademark disdain.

"Who else did he spend time with?"

"I have no idea."

"Where were you yesterday?"

"Your time's up, asshole," she said and signaled to a burly bouncer who hovered on the other side of the railing.

Red stalked off, and I tried to follow, but the bouncer blocked my path. "Wait," I called feebly, "I have thirty seconds left." But she was already at someone else's elbow.

"You're outta here, pal," said the bouncer, and in the time it takes to turn your head, I was gone.

TEN

In the Air Tonight

I was beginning to think my interview skills needed some brushing up. Baseless accusations were not producing the best results. Maybe Billy had run off with someone else, but there was no way I was getting back inside to find out. At least not tonight. And without a local lead, I'd either be off to Atlantic City or off the case. I ran a quick tab in my head and realized that if I quit now, I may have to refund some money, but if I went to Atlantic City, I could probably hit Miss Liz for another advance. Duh, hello. What's that choice again?

I sat in the car and stewed and took a closer look at the postcard from the Shore. The postmark was from Atlantic City, but the card was only addressed to "Boobsalot." It had been handwritten using a blue ball point and featureless block printing. What did that prove? Besides the fact that I would rather jump to conclusions than conduct in-depth interviews? I couldn't say for sure that Wayward Will had even sent the card because I never bothered to collect a sample of his writing. Time to regroup and develop Plan B. I called my client, but she wasn't exactly thrilled to hear from me. Who could blame her?

"Just what have you been doing with your time, Mr. Rotten? Besides meeting with my mother," she snapped.

I assured her I'd been making progress and then explained I had some physical evidence I needed her to authenticate.

"What evidence?"

"A note that may have been sent by your husband."

"What does it say?"

"I'm not even sure it is from your husband," I said. "I'd like you to take a look at the handwriting before we jump to any conclusions." If I didn't act like a professional, at least I could sound like one.

"Bring it over," was all she said before hanging up the phone. I could only assume she meant right away so I fired up the Toyota and headed back to the 'burbs.

I stopped at an E-Z Mart to top off my tank and empty my bladder. I combed my hair, dabbed at my bloodshot eyes with a damp towel, and tried to shake the smoke from my clothes. Feeling refreshed, I bought a soft pretzel and some Tic-Tacs and wondered what sort of relationship my client had with her mother. She knew about our meeting, and she'd sounded annoyed, but not too surprised. Can you get used to crap like that? And if Liz knew about the meeting, did she know about the old lady's offer to her husband? I thought not. Who'd put up with that? In any case, it was getting crowded behind the scenes. Some of these backstage shenanigans would have to move front and center soon.

I parked in the Gardners' driveway behind the same maroon Saab as the day before, but when I rang the bell, there was definitely a change in the air. A barking clamor swelled behind the door joined by two female voices—one, annoyed, the other, soothing. The soothing voice greeted me in the form of Alison Owen. Why wasn't I prepared for this? Did she ever *not* look lovely? After Casey's crack, I knew I'd be playing "Is-She-Or-Isn't-She?" the whole time I was there.

"Come on in," Alison said affably. "Don't mind the dogs. They won't bother you." The canine chorus consisted of a mongrel retriever, a rat terrier, and a whippet. "Now take a sniff, boys," she said to the hounds, "Then go lie down."

I crossed the threshold. The "boys" sniffed me up and down and then retreated obediently to the dining room.

"Good evening, Mr. Rotten," my client called from the couch. "You said something on the phone about a note."

"Yes, a postcard actually," I said as I crossed the room and offered her the card. "I think it may have been sent by your husband."

Mrs. Gardner was seated on the same couch as before but at a different angle. She was lounging today, with her feet up, facing the fireplace where a gas jet burned quietly, a wine glass within reach on a low table. Soft jazz played in the background. I was crashing cocktail time.

Alison closed the door and moved to the head of the couch. She caught my eye and raised her own empty glass from an end table while mouthing the words, "Want a drink?"

Of course I did, but I smiled and shook my head, and Alison made her way down the hall to the kitchen. She appeared to be quite at home.

"Is this a joke?" said Mrs. Gardner after she had inspected the card front and back. "Where did you get this?"

"From a dancer at that club," I answered as Alison returned with her glass of white wine and stood once again behind her friend. Liz handed her the postcard. "Is that your husband's handwriting?" I asked my client.

"His handwriting is terrible," said Liz. "That's why he started using that block printing in the classroom."

"So, you think that note may have been written by your husband?" I asked gently, mostly for Alison's sake. I wanted to show her how sensitive I could be, but Ms. Liz was having none of it.

"What are you suggesting, Mr. Rotten?"

"I'm not suggesting anything," I said. "I'm just trying to piece together what happened to your husband, and someone mentioned he was spending time at that club."

"What is this 'Boobsalot'?" she asked. "What kind of a club?"

"It's that strip joint over on Tremont," said Alison, unable to suppress a smile.

"Good lord," said Mrs. Gardner with a sigh. "And just who happened to mention this?"

"One of your husband's school colleagues."

"Which one?"

"Ann Deaver."

"Sweet Annie," said Liz with a touch of sarcasm. "And what else did she tell you?"

"Not a whole lot," I said, stalling. "Just that over the past few years your husband had lost some enthusiasm for his work."

"What did the slut say about me?" asked Liz with enough bite to bring a look of concern to Alison's eyes.

"I got the impression the two of you are not exactly best of friends," I said, trying to downplay the discord.

"Specifically, what did she say? Did she mention having seen me recently?"

"It's okay, Lizzie," said Alison, trying to ease the tension, but Liz wasn't backing off.

The expectant mother glared at me expectantly while Diana Krall crooned "Baby Baby All The Time" in the background. I knew what she was asking me, but I couldn't see how it would help to admit it. It would only piss her off to know that I knew, and she didn't seem too crazy about me to begin with. And I had promised Ann to keep it to myself.

"She said something like, 'Tell Liz I don't have her husband,'" I said, which was true. "'Tell Liz I don't *want* her husband.'"

"That bitch," snorted my client, shaking her head, but apparently, it was what she wanted to hear. She paused a moment and then resumed her interrogation. "What do you mean 'spending time'?" she asked.

"Excuse me?"

"At this 'Boobsalot.'"

"I don't know exactly how much time," I said, feeling less sensitive and sympathetic by the minute. "Enough time to be recognized by a few of the dancers. Enough time to be considered a regular."

"You went there and talked to these women?"

"Two of them, and the barmaid."

"And they knew Billy?"

"They didn't know his name, but they did know his face."

"That son of a bitch," she muttered. "He told me he was involved in some after-school tutoring program."

"Take it easy, Elizabeth," said Alison as she gently patted her friend's shoulder. "Remember what the doctor said." Like maybe, you shouldn't be drinking wine if you're preggers.

"Goddamit!" said Liz and then she shook off Alison's hand and got up to pace behind the couch. Alison set her wine glass on the mantel and tried to console her friend in such a way that had me leaning toward the notion that I was, unfortunately, *not* Alison's type.

"It's time to let the loser go, Elizabeth," cooed Alison in Liz' ear.

"It's time to cut his balls off," muttered Liz savagely. She then took a moment to compose herself before turning back to me. "What else did you find out?" she asked quietly as she resumed her seat on the couch.

"Not a whole lot," I said and then moved on briskly to avoid becoming a target. "That card may have been a joke. It's not addressed to anyone in particular, and there was no talk of missing dancers at the club. I spoke with the people at the travel agency. Your husband did take the bus down with the group. He apparently won a lot of money playing craps, and he was last seen gambling in one of the casinos. They waited half an hour on Sunday morning, and they checked his room, but when he didn't show up, they left without him."

"Was he with anyone?"

"He traveled down alone, and he was the only one who missed the bus back," I said, but I had run out of stall. "At the casino, he was apparently with a professional escort."

"That bastard!" she said and then buried her face in her hands. Alison shot me a dirty look and then massaged her friend's shoulders. "That lying sack of shit!" continued my client who got up to pace again behind the couch. "I won't let him leave me this way. He'll come back and do this right. Fucking weasel, after all the years I carried him."

Ms. Liz had wandered into the dining room where she picked up a book from the table and threw it down the hall with a strangled shout of exasperation. The retriever trotted off dutifully in the direction of the thud and returned with mouth full and tail wagging.

Liz burst into tears, and Alison held her in her arms and stroked her hair. The dog sat patiently at their feet, and I searched for an excuse to be someplace else. And yet my client seemed uncomfortable with her friend's physical displays of affection, at least in front of me. She recovered quickly and turned to me with updated instructions.

"You find the bastard and tell him if he doesn't come back and do the right thing, he'll end up with nothing. Less than nothing. He'll be paying me."

"I'll leave for Atlantic City tonight," I said, then paused before adding, "But I'll need some additional expense money." Alison frowned, and my client stared blankly. "Two-fifty should do," I said, and Liz walked off down the hall.

Alison crossed to the mantel and downed half her glass of wine in one gulp. "I appreciate your discretion, Mr. Rotten, but don't push things too far. My offer still stands. I'll calm her down. The last thing she needs right now is to have him back in her life."

Liz returned with the check and showed me out. I didn't mention Phil Cheswick's free ride, but I did promise to call her from the Shore.

"And if my mother contacts you again," she said as I stepped onto the stoop, "Just remember who you're working for."

I remembered all the way down to the bank, but once the check was deposited, I figured I was working for myself.

ELEVEN

Give It Up or Let Me Go

Ugly, ugly, ugly. Why couldn't two people just say, "Hey, this ain't working out," and move on? I'm not saying you should be friends for life or anything, but why make such a big deal out of it? Why put so much energy and emotion into beating up on somebody you used to love? I've had my share of bad break-ups, but I usually find a way to get past it. Then again, I'm not certain my exes all felt the same way. Maybe someone was out there holding a grudge. Maybe I'm just a shallow individual. People are all hung up on retribution, is what it is. You done me wrong, you dirty rat, and now you're gonna pay. We want people to be prosecuted for crimes of the heart. And if public justice is not forthcoming, we take matters into our own hands. Or we hire someone like me. Oh, well. All aboard for America's Playground.

It occurred to me on the drive home that I should pack a change of clothes and maybe a toothbrush. This would be my first professional trip out of town. I'd have to work out a special rate schedule. Should I charge around the clock? Could I expense all my meals? Jim Rockford didn't often leave LA, so I was on my own, and the camcorders were starting to dance.

I stopped and bought a bunch of travel-sized toiletries and a few magazines to read on the bus. Then I drove home, parked in my usual spot down a side street, and walked around to my apartment. I was so involved in mental preparations for my trip that I didn't notice Ann Deaver till I practically bumped into her. She stood in the middle of the sidewalk facing my front door. She was holding something in her hand as she searched for the house number that wasn't there.

"Hey, what are *you* doing here?" I said in typically witty fashion.

"Oh, Mr. Rotten. I was looking for you, but I couldn't find your number," she said, disarmingly confused.

"The guy downstairs is in hiding. Every time the landlord replaces the number, the nutcase takes it down. I think he throws them in the river. How about calling me 'Frank'?"

"Call me 'Ann,' Frank," she said with a smile.

"How did you even know what number to look for?" My cards only listed my phone number, and most of my business mail went to my PO box.

"I spoke with your partner," Ann said and I assumed she meant Des. I suppose I should have been pissed, but if he kept sending alluring women my way, I could learn to live with his meddling.

"I got this card in the mail today," she continued, handing me a postcard of some big-ass elephant staring out to sea. "And I also wanted to apologize for my attitude yesterday. I was a little hard on Billy. I wasn't having a very good day."

"No problem," I said, and meant it. The card was addressed to "Annie Deaver" but, once again, wasn't signed. It simply read, "Having a great time. Wish you were here."

"You think Gardner sent this card?"

"That's his printing. And he used to talk about that elephant. Used to be a hotel. It's near the place he stayed on his gambling trips."

"He sent this to your home?"

"Yes," she said, leaving me to wonder, again, about the nature of their relationship. "I called that place," she added, snapping me back, "But he wasn't registered. At least not under his own name."

"What place is that?"

"The Shifting Sands Motor Inn. It's actually a little south of Atlantic City."

"You've been there? You've been on these trips?"

"I have *not* taken one of those trips," she said with a touch of attitude returning. "Billy would tell me about them." She took a breath and then continued in a softer tone. "We've had playground duty together for the past five years. You hear a lot about a person's life, whether you want to or not."

"I'm leaving for Atlantic City tonight," I said, and I almost asked her to go with me.

"I hope you find him."

"You want to come up for a beer?" I asked on impulse.

"No, thank you," she replied with the barest hint of a blush. "I just wanted to drop off the card. And I think I gave you the impression yesterday that I didn't care what happened to Billy, but I do, and I'm starting to worry. I just get frustrated with him at times. He's really quite good in the classroom, but that doesn't seem to be enough for him."

"What more does he want?"

"I don't know. I'm not sure *he* knows. He doesn't even realize what he's got," she said in exasperation and then paused thoughtfully before concluding, "Everybody wants to be a bright light these days, but some very good work is being done in the shadows."

"I'm sure there is," I said, though I wasn't quite sure what she was talking about.

She promised to give me a call if she heard from Gardner again; then she wished me luck and disappeared around the same corner the Rolls had earlier in the day. I thought about chasing after her, but then I thought about how silly I'd look, and I didn't. I let the moment pass and then made my way up the stairs. Trudy was waiting on the second-floor landing.

"Another hard day at the office, dear?" she asked.

"Hey, Trude. 'Take a sad song and make it better.' God, I'm beat. Women been shaking their tits in my face all day."

"You've got no couth, Frank," she said shaking her head, "And that woman on the sidewalk wasn't 'shaking her tits.'"

"No fair peeking. You been checking up on me?"

"Somebody has to," she said, and she was probably right.

"I had to go back to that go-go joint again," I told her, trying to change the subject, but she was not to be deterred.

"Who was that woman downstairs, then? Your client or her girlfriend?"

"Neither. Friend and colleague of my missing man. She's a schoolteacher. She got a postcard too," I said, but I didn't feel like explaining further, so I tried again to change the subject. "Hey, you want to go to Atlantic City? You can be my escort for the weekend. I'll put you on my expense account."

"Jerk," was her only reply.

"What are you doing for dinner?" I asked.

"I've got no plans."

"Wanna go out?"

"I've got no money either."

I thought for a moment. "Let me stash this stuff upstairs and see what Des is doing. Back in a jiff."

Des was home but in the bathroom. Rather than shout through the door, I took a moment to check my messages, of which I had one. Karen Stanley wanted to know what I was doing for dinner, but when I called her office, she'd already left for the day, and I realized I didn't have her home number. Did this mean our relationship was strictly professional?

"Hey, Karen," I said to her office recorder, "Sorry I missed your call. I'm off to Atlantic City for the weekend. Talk to you Monday. Ciao, baby," I added for effect.

As soon as I set the receiver down, the phone rang again.

"Hel-lo-o, baby," I said, aping the Big Bopper, thinking it would be Karen.

"Good evening, Mister Rotten," said Ramona Taft. "I understand you're leaving for Atlantic City tonight."

"News travels fast."

"Some events unfold rather slowly," she said, putting me in my place. "Now, what can you tell me about this Alison Owen?"

"She's a friend of your daughter's."

"What kind of friend?"

"A very close friend, by the looks of it," I said, giving her something to think about.

"I may have another job for you when you get back," she said without providing any specifics. "Let me know when you locate Mister Gardner, whether he intends to accept my offer or not."

She gave me a number where she could be reached over the weekend, and then off she was, to the club, or some such place where rich people sit around and brag about all the deals they've turned and chains they've yanked that day. Hey, sign me up, sounds like fun.

"Hey, I thought you were going to Atlantic City?" said Des, emerging from his ablutions.

"I'm leaving tonight, about eleven-thirty. Say, what're you doing for dinner?"

Des had no plans, and he was hungry, but he had no cash, and I wasn't about to bankroll a banquet for three. We searched the cupboards and found a jar of fancy clam sauce that was still a few months shy of expiring, and a box of linguini. Des agreed to do some dishes, Trudy offered to make a salad, and I went on a wine and bread run. Within forty-five minutes, the three of us were smiling at plates of steaming pasta while sitting at the big oak table which had come with our apartment. I was trying to sell the seat beside me on the Casino Express, but no one was buying.

"C'mon, Trude. You'll love being an escort. You get to dress up, hang out, and spend a lot of time with *me*."

"No way, sicko," she said. "Sounds pretty sleazy, not to mention boring. Besides, I've got a date tomorrow."

"Another night out with Dreamboat Manny, the Eligible Orphan?"

"You betcha," said Trudy, smiling.

"How 'bout you, Des?" I said, still selling. "I'll bet you could use some excitement in your life."

"Losing money doesn't excite me," said Des. "And there's no way I'm missing Rodolfo's bash." He paused to swallow, and I silently accepted defeat. "You really think you'll find that guy?" he asked while loading another forkful.

"I don't know, but I don't really have much choice about going down there. If I bailed out now, I'd have to refund some money, and my client is majorly pissed. She wants to see this guy suffer."

"Well, he sounds like a total asshole," said Trudy.

"I guess he does," I said, "But we *are* only getting half the story."

"You *would* defend a total pig."

"I'm not defending him. I just don't know. And what happened to innocent until proven guilty?"

"That only applies to guys who are actually innocent," said Trudy. "And this guy is obviously an asshole."

"Why's a guy like that run off anyway?" said Des.

"His friend thinks he's not satisfied being a schoolteacher," I said. "He wants to do something more high profile, but he's not sure what it is."

"Like gambling?" asked Trudy.

"I don't know. Gambling *is* a bit tacky, but what happens if you never figure out what you want to do with your life? What then?"

"You probably end up doing what somebody else wants you to do," said Des.

"Like having babies," added Trudy.

"Who's having a baby?" asked Des.

"My client, the missing man's wife. His teacher friend thinks that's what pushed him over the edge."

"Sounds like a mid-life crisis to me," said Des.

"How was it, again, you found out this woman was pregnant?" asked Trudy.

"I got it from a reliable source."

"But she never, like, said to you, 'I'm having a baby and my husband can't handle it'?"

"She tap dances around the truth, but I know she's hiding something."

"Maybe it's not *his* kid," said Trudy.

"She's having an affair with a *woman*," I reminded her. "It has to be somebody's baby."

"There are ways, Frank," said Trudy.

"Too weird," I said, wondering exactly what I had slept through in biology class.

"Well, it doesn't seem to make much sense," said Des who appeared to be giving the matter some serious thought. "He had just about everything a guy like that could want. Wife, nice house, steady job. Why wouldn't he want kids?"

"Too much responsibility?" I said.

"He's already a teacher," said Des. "They have to be pretty responsible."

"Too selfish," said Trudy with a snort.

"Maybe something did happen to him," said Des.

"Maybe he got kidnapped," said Trudy, tongue slightly in cheek.

"Or abducted by aliens," said Des, displaying the effects of too many talk shows.

"Maybe he just got fed up," I said, knowing a little something about the subject.

"I'm sticking with mid-life crisis," said Des. "They're big with Boomers these days."

"Ooohh, dropping out is so-o-o sixties," cooed Trudy.

"What do you know about the sixties?" I asked, fed up with the nostalgia for a time none of us had ever known.

"I was *born* in the sixties," said Trudy.

"I didn't know you were that old," I teased.

"Don't be such a pig. Besides, I took that course." Trudy had taken a course in college called "Making Sense of the Sixties."

"Well, he *is* old," I said. "He went to Woodstock."

"Which one?" asked Des.

"Well, not the one that just happened."

"The first one?" said Des, moderately impressed but still skeptical. "Nineteen sixty-nine?"

"He's got his tickets framed and hanging on his wall."

"God, he *is* a fossil," said Trudy, but that was about all we could agree on—some old guy was missing and his wife wanted him back. Motivation remained a mystery. And yet, I was getting paid to locate a loser and deliver a message, not solve a riddle.

After dinner, Trudy retired to her studio to paint, and Des got ready for work. He was bartending at the Row from eight to two and then swabbing the decks till dawn. Better him than me. I couldn't work that hard to make a living. I showered and packed, then brewed a pot of coffee, and watched part of the Woodstock movie which Des had on tape. I made a game out of looking for Billy Gardner among the fresh-faced, spaced-out kids who were convinced they were witnessing history and about to change the world. I could imagine him weighing less, with longer hair and blue jeans, maybe a head band, but I couldn't find room for his jaded cynicism amid all that babbling, hopeful innocence. Nobody talked like that anymore. The times they had a-changed.

TWELVE

Hit the Road, Jack

As I drove to meet the motor coach, the reality of my commitment closed in. I would soon be on my way to America's Playground. An all-night ride would bring us to the casinos around mid-morning, after stopping for breakfast, then most in the group would begin gambling their savings away, while I went off in search of a single sand flea on the back of a St. Bernard. What made people think I could find this guy? It seemed like the longest of long shots to me, but sleeping on a bus beat swabbing the deck at Desolation Row, even if I was destined to wake in New Jersey.

I parked my car with the others and quickly realized that I had arrived late for my lost weekend. The bus had already boarded and was idling impatiently in front of Cheswick Travel. Terry, the reluctant receptionist, had morphed into Tour Group Coordinator—a frustrated young woman wielding a clipboard, but kinda hot. She was scanning the sidewalk for stragglers as I approached.

"Phil lets you have all the fun," I quipped lamely as I prepared to board.

"You're late," she said, and then added a warning. "Give me any shit and Earl will bounce your butt off the bus." Earl was the burly bus driver who grinned menacingly from his pneumatic seat.

I promised to behave and climbed up to the center aisle. The bus was about half-full, but a lot of people seemed to be traveling together, so I found a pair of empty seats about midway back and plopped down next to the window. I'm not much for chatting with strangers under the best of circumstances, but the brief survey of my fellow excursionists had convinced me to seek sleep immediately. Toothless retirees sat across from Marla Maples wannabees. A cluster of Slick Vinnie corner boys postured and preened for the Marlas, while a pair of collegiate dweebs prepared to test their statistical gaming theories. Rounding out the group was an unwitting Elvis impersonator with gold charms and chest hair on display. I was adrift on a sea of addled expectation. I looked to Terry for a lifeline, but she ignored my plight and took a seat near the front. She made a few notes on her clipboard and scanned the sidewalk one last time before giving Earl the go-ahead.

I slouched with lids lowered as the bus made its way along the river to the highway and out to the Turnpike, but my eyes inadvertently bounced open when we stopped at the toll booth for our ticket and the night owl across the aisle nailed me.

"What's your game, young fella?" asked the old codger swathed in shadow.

"Say what?"

"Blackjack? Craps? Roulette?"

"I'm not sure," I said, but his query gave me pause. What *was* my game? It had never occurred to me that I should be asking questions of people on the bus, and now this sleepless old man was turning the tables.

"I stick with the slots, myself," he said. "You lose slower that way."

"Leave the man alone, Sy," said the lumpy woman beside him without opening her eyes.

Sy waved her objection away, but I didn't give him the chance to begin again. "I'm looking for someone," I said.

"On the bus?" he asked in a softer voice as he looked around at the other passengers.

"In Atlantic City."

"Someone who lives down there?"

"Someone who *went* down there last week and didn't come back."

"On the bus?"

"On the bus," I said.

"Who?"

"Guy named Billy Gardner."

"I don't know from names, but I was on the bus last week."

"Older guy, about forty-two," I said. "Medium build, dark hair, dopey face."

"I don't know about the dopey face," said Sy, "But the school-teacher's the only one didn't come back. He played blackjack and craps."

"You knew him?"

"Only from the bus. I know most of the regulars."

"That him?" I asked, displaying Gardner's snapshot.

"That's him."

"So what happened to him?"

"Who knows?" said Sy with a shrug. "Nice guy, but sometimes people miss the bus."

"He never came home."

"Never? From last week?" he said with a hint of concern. "He's still down there?"

"We're not sure," I said. "Nobody's really heard from him." I wasn't counting the postcards.

Sy blinked soberly behind thick-lensed glasses. "He was not a happy person, the teacher," said the old man in confidence. "I don't think he knew what he wanted from life. Anything could have happened."

"Sy, what a thing to say," scolded the lump. "Now get some sleep."

Sy shrugged again and settled in beside his wife. I wondered if I was sitting in the teacher's seat and shuddered at the thought of being a regular on this bus. A tad too existential for my tastes. I checked the emergency exits and then tossed a glance Terry's way, but she was chatting quietly with Earl, so I stared out the window at nothing much passing by. I hadn't considered the fact that Gardner might be lying someplace cold with a tag on his toe, but I couldn't shake Sy's gloomy assessment. Old people spend too much time reading obituaries and those oddball stories that flesh out the midsections of most big-city newspapers. "Man Loses Legs in Kitchen Mishap" or "Woman Crushed by Piano in Empty Club." Something like that happens maybe once a year in a city the size of Pittsburgh, but people read about it every day. Nowhere to run and nowhere to hide, baby. Except, maybe, Atlantic City.

I pulled out one of my magazines and scanned a few of the empty-headed articles squeezed between endless ads for clothes, booze, and cologne. Now here was something that happened every day—chasing tail and getting trashed. Sex, drugs, and smelling good—that's what life was all about. Reconnected with reality, I drifted off to sleep as we sped through the timeless black tunnel of south-central Pennsylvania.

I slept through to the next tollbooth, west of Philadelphia, where we ditched the Turnpike for the Schuylkill Expressway. I awoke stiff and unrested with my tongue glued to the roof of my mouth. The sun was barely working its way up, and most of my fellow sufferers were still asleep, except for Sy, who sat quietly beside his wife and smiled my way when I began to stir.

"How much longer?" I asked as I attempted to stretch in the cramped space between seats.

"Couple of hours," he said quietly. "We stop for breakfast first."

"How long before breakfast?"

"About an hour."

I blinked out the window at the scenery beginning to form in the dim dawn light. I didn't know exactly what was out there, but I didn't like the looks of it. There was nothing familiar, and this was no place I wanted to be—on a bus, sliding inexorably into New Jersey. How's that song go, "It's like Ohio, but even more so, imagine that." Just imagine.

I was having serious second thoughts about my chosen profession. The camcorders had stopped dancing. How could I be expected to find someone when I felt lost half the time myself? I was up too early, and I knew it, but there was nothing I could do about it. I should have been addressing my insecurities in dreams, but the bus wouldn't let me back to sleep. I craved a cup of coffee but settled for the sight of the Philadelphia Art Museum perched on a bluff above the Schuylkill. River, that is. Finally, something familiar, courtesy of Sly Stallone and the Thanksgiving Day parade. Then Veteran's Stadium rose up and the city skyline I'd seen via the Goodyear blimp. Not quite the answer to all life's questions, but enough certified reality to restore my sense of perspective. And none too soon, for as we crossed the Delaware, I realized that New Jersey did, in fact, resemble Ohio. Say, the outskirts of Youngstown or Dayton. Housing developments built on former farmland viewed from a divided highway. For a while I could have been a lot of places where the same scenario had played out—Illinois, Virginia, Minnesota, Indiana, Iowa; was there a place it hadn't happened? But eventually we found some working farms, and they were growing berries, not corn, and we left Ohio behind. We traded buckeyed chestnuts for pinecones, and I understood why some people worked so hard to preserve some things. And yet I wasn't exactly disappointed when I started seeing signs for Burger King, for I knew just what to expect and how long it would take to get there.

We stopped at a service plaza named for a past political kingpin. Nothing poetic about the AC Expressway. I got juice and coffee, and a couple of Breakfast Buddies then wandered out and ate in the wooded picnic area. The world had stopped vibrating, and cars passed in isolated *whooshes* in place of the constant rumble of the bus. It was almost like a little nature preserve. Birds chirped in the trees, and something rustled through the underbrush. Someone had even gone to the trouble of putting name tags on the trees. If it hadn't been for the key-chain dice in the gift shop and the deadbeats sleeping in their cars, you could almost forget you were on the outskirts of something sordid. But not for long. Terry herded us back on the bus, and we were underway within an hour.

I flopped back by my window, still sullen but no longer schizoid, and flipped through the free entertainment weekly I'd picked up inside. On paper, at least, Atlantic City had the look of one of those "no there there" places. The rag was all ads—no reviews, no articles, no advice columns. And no ads for futons, coffee shops, or bookstores. Two pages of escort ads in place of personals. I guess no one stayed in town long enough to settle down and start a relationship. Lots of restaurants and bars, but mostly cover bands for entertainment. No "names" outside the casinos, and those names belonged to celebrity impersonators, illusionists, current country performers, and fossilized rock 'n' rollers. Formerly big names like Crosby, Stills, and Nash had gone from cutting edge to casino showroom in a Boomer lifetime. A simple case of take-the-money-and-run, but it was enough to make people like Casey Conlon puke. I couldn't wait to tell her.

I set the paper aside, but looking out the window wasn't much better. The Atlantic City skyline grew Oz-like on the horizon, providing the backdrop for an army of enormous billboards that had invaded the surrounding marshland. Hot babes blew on big dice. Acres and acres of quarter slots and bulging buffets awaited. Giant Todd Rundgrens and Ringo Starrs smiled down as we began our final approach. What's the joke, guys? And who the hell is Freddie Roman? Just when I thought things couldn't get grosser, we were shunted from the Expressway and descended another level. Bridge construction forced us onto a secondary route which passed through a breeding ground for serial killers. Rundown motels offering hourly rates alternated with razor-wired parking lots and discount liquor stores. A garishly clad woman stumbled out of a taxicab holding a single shoe. A man clutching a brown-bagged bottle gestured dramatically to no one. And this was daylight. Imagine what went on when the sun went down. This strip might have seemed futuristic in its fifties hey-day, but the future was now. Another piece of disposable culture offering inspiration to science fiction scenarists. Or maybe I had it wrong. Maybe this was part of some new "theme park" casino. Say, Bally's Blade Runner by the Bay?

"This used to be the main road into the city," said Sy with a sigh from across the aisle. "Look at it now." He paused and shook his head sadly before adding, "Of course, before casinos, it all looked like this."

Hard to believe, but maybe they'd saved this stretch as a reminder, or a rebuttal whenever anyone asked why the city had sold its soul. Something to generate a little sympathy for the devil. Whatever. Before long, we were stop-starting our way through a more conventional city scape and soon arrived at our destination. We'd made our way through the desert and disembarked at the door to the promised land. Milk and honey waited inside, and everyone raced to redeem their coupons.

The coupon quest drew us onto the casino floor which resembled an enormous mall anchor store with Decor by Dementia. I queued up with the others for my starter roll of quarters. All around us lights flashed, bells sounded, and coins clattered in slot trays—the siren song of easy money. Stuff ten in, the machine returns five, and by gamblers' logic you've become a "winner." I walked away from the change counter and got sucked into the gaming table maze. I looked around and found no clocks, no windows, and no apparent way out. I wasn't ready for this right now. The room was closing in, and I had this irrational desire to float away. The solid weight of the quarter roll provided ballast, and I knew if I cracked the wrapper, I'd be gone. It took fifteen minutes, but I finally broke free and found daylight, on the Famous Boardwalk. The grand wooden way, Monopoly's highest-priced property—part park, part thoroughfare, thoroughly weird. A carnival midway where sideshow locals auditioned for a sequel to *Freaks*. Drag queens distributed leaflets to strolling seniors, swarms of pigeons descended on peanut eaters, and the stump of a woman prone on a gurney blew out a barely discernible harmonica tune. Drop some change in her cup and make a request. It all sounds the same. Slender men pushed stout women in rolling basket chairs. Vendors hawked hot dogs, T-shirts, fudge, and flip-flops. Madame Edith promised spiritual advice, and her services were sorely needed. If my client wanted to punish her spouse, she'd let him stay lost right here.

I stumbled to the beach rail and blinked stupidly at the dull gray carpet that stretched to the horizon. Ripples moved through the rug and foam formed at its edge. The ocean. I'd forgotten about the freaking ocean! The Atlantic, right? So damn big and you don't see it till you're practically in it. All that water, those mysterious depths, the uncontrolled open space—an imposing incongruity. And what an enormous distraction! Must drive those casino guys nuts. You can't own it and can't alter it, so they tried to hide it. All the new construction had been designed to ignore or obscure any appreciation of natural beauty. Towering technicolor minarets pulled the eye away from the gently lapping waves. Vast windowless walls dulled the senses, and an inverse status system had been installed—bums slept under the boardwalk, while the highest rollers were kept as far from the water as possible. Mondo America—the worst aspects of modern culture reflected in a fun house mirror. And Billy Gardner had embraced this environment, had returned time and again, and had apparently lost himself here. What was I to do? Stop the strollers and show his picture? My client had been reluctant to involve the boys and girls in blue, but I couldn't see a better place to start. I took Casey Conlon's advice and stopped in a convenience store where I picked up a local map and directions to the police station.

For all the attention it received, the city was geographically compact, so I set out on foot. That first block off the boards was a long, lonely stretch of decay, and the first cross street, Pacific Avenue, with its parking lots, motels, and pawn shops, was little more than a casino service road. But beyond that I found the typical, jive-ass, rundown rhythm of the inner city. Boom boxes blared, traffic snarled, street vendors sold what they could. Oddly enough, real people lived here. But why? Heading west, I crossed Atlantic, the Avenue, and couldn't miss the imposing, black-walled City Hall which also housed the police department. I had to walk halfway around to find my way in, but I soon discovered that I was not the first out-of-town investigator who'd come looking for a lost soul.

"Sergeant Harris, third floor," said the uniformed officer who manned the metal detector when I asked for the missing persons' department.

I took the elevator up and found Sgt. Alberta Harris behind the Detectives' Duty Desk. She wasn't exactly happy to see me. Another woman in love with her work.

"You a relative?" she asked after I explained why I was there.

"I'm a private investigator hired by the missing man's wife."

"She file a missing person's report?"

"No, not yet."

"Well, she should," said Sgt. Harris. "That's as much as we can do—match up the reports with the bodies on hand." She paused a moment to let the advice sink in and then asked, "What's this guy look like?"

I described William Gardner and showed Alberta his picture. She frowned and shook her head as she pulled a worn photo album from under the counter. "I don't believe we have anybody here right now who fits that description," she said after flipping through the book, which she then turned around to give me a look.

Polaroid snapshots of dead men were arranged neatly, two to a page. Each was labeled "John Doe" (no "Janes" in this book) with a number. The numbers ran into double digits. None even remotely resembled my missing schoolteacher.

"All these bodies are in the morgue right now?" I asked in disbelief.

"Just the first three pages. If they're not identified after a month, they're cremated at county expense." When I frowned, she added, "Point being, people like your Mister Gardner don't often end up in this book. He'd be on the streets a few years before he made it in here."

"Any patients in the hospital who haven't been identified?"

"I wouldn't know about those," she said. "You'd have to check the medical center. On Pacific."

"This town have a homeless shelter?"

"There's the Mission, behind the new convention center," she said, sounding a little impatient. "Have you checked under the Boardwalk?"

I couldn't tell if she was serious about that last bit, but I sensed she had better things to do with her time than chat with some tourist. So, I did my best to look pathetic and stupid, which wasn't much of a stretch for me, and she showed a little sympathy, sort of.

"You say your guy missed a tour bus or something?" she said.

"Yeah, last weekend."

"Sometimes when they lose all their money, they get too embarrassed to go home," she said, opening up. "And if he was looking to get lost, he sure picked the right place. This is a city full of strangers. He wouldn't need much money to hole up in one of those flea bags out on the Pike."

Checking all those motels was more than I could do in a day, and I wasn't looking to stretch this adventure out. Besides, they didn't call them "no-tell" motels for nothing. Sgt. Harris sensed my malaise and sent me on my way with some more advice. "You tell that woman to just wait," she said. "He'll find his way home. Stray dogs usually do."

I thanked Sgt. Harris for her help and found my way back to the street, feeling more like a detective, even if my efforts were proving futile.

THIRTEEN

Let's Get Lost

The odds were getting longer that I'd find Billy Gardner, but I resolved to go through the motions anyway. Besides, what else was I going to do all day in Atlantic City? Gamble? That seemed to be about it for this town at this time of year—roll the dice or walk the streets.

I walked back to Pacific and took a jitney, a cross between a cab and a bus, down to the hospital. Believe it or not, they actually had a wing named after Frank Sinatra. What did they treat there? Chronic swagger? Overbearing attitude? Jilly Rizzo disorder? Rat Pack syndrome? I imagined myself calling Miz Liz to tell her I found her husband in the Frank Sinatra Wing, but it was not meant to be. The hospital did house two unidentified patients, but they were both Crazy Janes—schizophrenic, homeless women. There were two other area hospitals, on the mainland, and I called them both, but neither had any nameless guests. Apparently, that was a problem they only had in the city. Everybody in suburbia knew who they were.

I wandered back cross town with the Mission in mind, but I got stalled in a blocks-square wasteland that resembled Europe after the war. Pick a war, any war. Acre after city acre had been reduced to rubble as part of something called "The Gateway Project," the goal of which appeared to be knocking down anything that blocked one's view of the casino parking garages when entering the city on the Expressway. In a car. It took twenty minutes to detour the deconstruction site, and another ten to work my way around the shell of the new convention center which deliberately displayed its backside to the Mission and the dilapidated neighborhood that surrounded it. To be sure, you wouldn't expect to find a place like the Mission in a nice neighborhood, and you wouldn't want conventioneers wandering off and getting mugged, but did they really need to be so obvious with their symbolism?

The Mission was not the flophouse I thought it would be. It was staffed largely by young, committed, Christian volunteers, and all the occupants had identities. And children. The place was set up to serve homeless families who pledged serious intent to improve their lives and attend religious services. There were no accommodations for single males, or atheists or Muslims, except in emergency situations, like bitter cold or a hurricane. Acute embarrassment and extreme disaffection did not qualify as emergencies. I declined the opportunity to make a monetary contribution—that worship requirement didn't sit right—and hit the bricks before someone tried to save me. My meager agenda exhausted, I drifted lazily toward the beach, sidestepping construction debris and wending my way through idling bus traffic. I poked my head into a few go-go joints on Pacific, but there wasn't much shaking so early in the afternoon. I snagged a dog from a sidewalk vendor and made my way back to the Boardwalk beach rail, eating as I walked. Just for the hell of it I climbed down to the sand and peered beneath the boards. Damn if there weren't people living down there, but they weren't friendly people, and they weren't happy to see me. I didn't stay long, and I didn't care much about finding Billy Gardner anymore. I only cared about killing time till the bus returned to take us to the . . . motel! To the same motel where Billy Gardner had stayed. My grasp of the obvious was slipping. Must be something in the sea air. I found the postcard with the address for the Shifting Sands Motor Inn, then hopped a cab, and headed down beach.

I had been wondering where the nice areas of Atlantic City were, and the answer seemed to be "out of town." Once south of the old, abandoned high school, the avenue opened up, and we crossed into Ventnor where the homes had more of a middle-class look. Margate was even more upscale with gaudy oceanfront villas and hundreds of newly constructed condo units. The Shifting Sands itself was a well-preserved relic of early sixties car culture, its most prominent features being its neon sign and its parking lot. But I didn't care what the place looked like as long as I had the chance to ask a few questions before the bus arrived. I entered the time capsule lobby and approached the front desk. A young dude was at work behind a translucent glass partition while a television tuned to MTV anachronistically blared in a corner. Whatever happened to *American Bandstand*? I tapped my fingers on the Formica countertop till the desk clerk acknowledged that he was no longer alone and peered around the partition.

"What's up?" he said distractedly. "I mean, welcome to the Shifting Sands. What can I do for you today?" It was obvious I was interrupting something, but he was making an effort.

"I'm with the group that's arriving later," I began, and with that the dude dropped the effort.

"The rooms aren't ready yet," he said and turned back to his translucent refuge.

"I don't want a room," I said. "I just want to ask a few questions."

He popped out to say, "The bus will be here soon," and then tried to duck back, but I wouldn't let him.

"I know the bus will be here soon. Why the hell you think I took a cab down here ahead of time?" I said, trying to impress on him that I was prepared to be a bigger asshole than he was. He relented and gave me his divided attention.

"Do you work these tours every weekend?" I asked.

"Every weekend," he replied glumly. "Mostly by myself."

"You remember anything in particular about last week's group?"

He surprisingly appeared to give it some thought before replying, "No."

"You remember seeing this guy?" I asked, showing him Gardner's picture.

He took a brief look and again answered, "No."

"This guy used to come down quite often. You sure you haven't seen him before?"

"I don't usually see the individual guests. I mostly deal directly with the group leaders," he said and then reached behind the glass for an ice bucket of room keys which he dropped on the counter. "This lobby isn't big enough to handle a whole group all at once. I give the keys and the room assignments to the leaders, and they give them out right on the bus. The people go straight from the bus to their rooms. They don't come through the lobby."

He was right about the lobby. Any more than ten people would be a tight fit.

"You work when they leave too?"

"Yes, I'll be here tomorrow morning," he replied wearily. "Check-out time is noon."

"What happens when someone misses the bus?"

"I don't know. The group leaders handle things like that."

"What if someone leaves stuff in the room?"

"Then the maid packs it up, and we hold it at the desk till someone comes for it."

"Anybody leave anything behind last weekend?"

"I really don't remember. There's nothing back here now," he said, and I knew he was giving me the bare minimum, and likely that's all there was. "Excuse me," he continued, "But that bus will be here any minute and I've got to get these keys ready."

"Yeah, sure," I said and then asked, "Hey, you know where I can get a cup of coffee?" I wasn't trying to be a pain in the ass, but I could feel myself starting to flag.

"That coffee maker is all set up," he said, waving over the top of the partition to a cart at the end of the counter. "Just press the button."

I did as instructed and in five minutes had a fresh cup of joe and as much outdated MTV as I could stand. I probably should have tried to track down the maids who'd been working last weekend, but I couldn't get motivated. It was weird to think that Bouncing Bill had been here just a week ago, maybe even came into the lobby for a cup of coffee, watched some MTV, and then simply wandered off somewhere. What would Rod Serling say? Had Sweet Bill slipped into the Twilight Zone? The answer may have been out there somewhere, but I'd done my bit, and I was ready to give it a rest and let this mystery be. For now.

I left the lobby and decided to take a stroll while I was waiting for the bus. I passed a club on the corner, then a ten-story condo, a parking lot, and an Italian restaurant before coming face-to-flank with that "big-ass" elephant from Louis Malle's movie and "Annie" Deaver's postcard. "Lucy," they called her, and she stood about four stories tall and gazed longingly out to sea, in the direction of the rising sun, I supposed. Which meant that her butt end faced the sidewalk where I stood. A sign said the old girl had been built in the Victorian era by some real estate developer. Big surprise. Then it had been used as a hotel before falling into disrepair and eventually being restored through the loving efforts of the "Save Lucy Committee"—what passed for community service in an affluent tourist town. What, no poor people around? How about dear old Mother Nature? She could use some help. No, man, no dunes. They block the view. Let's just fix up Lucy. Ain't we wonderful?

It certainly was a curiosity, and I couldn't help but wonder what the designer had in mind when he flipped the tail to one side and putt a four-paned window where Lucy's butt hole would have been. Victorian bathroom humor? Unfortunately, the big girl was only open in season so my question would remain unanswered until at least next spring. I was about to set off in search of other architectural oddities when I heard our bus approaching down the avenue and made my way back to the motel to meet it. Terry was first off and popped into the lobby for the keys, but room assignments weren't ready yet, and she emerged empty-handed. My fault, I suppose, for distracting the desk clerk.

"How's it going?" I asked as she prepared to reboard the bus. She was getting cuter all the time.

"Was that your idea of a joke?" she said as I approached. "Missing the bus like that?"

I hadn't thought about it before, but it was pretty funny. "No, no way," I assured her. "Hey, I'm sorry. I wasn't thinking. I'm not much of a gambler so I just decided to come down here and check things out before the crowd arrived."

She eyed me suspiciously and raised her foot to the first step.

"Hey, maybe we could have a drink together later? Let me make it up to you?" I said.

"I think not," she said as she stepped up beside Earl, but I didn't take it personal. The natives were getting restless, and she had to keep them in their seats, or close by, until the rooms were ready.

The Marlas stayed on the bus, but the Vinnies had to smoke. A few couples drifted down to the bulkhead for a glimpse of the sea, while some of the seniors who knew the routine stepped inside the lobby for coffee. I lingered by the side of the bus and wondered if I should roll the dice and ask Terry to dinner. I was debating the odds when old Sy's wife lumbered over with her reluctant spouse in tow.

"Tell the young man what you saw today," she said, prodding Sy, and I prepared myself for a Jerry Vale or Joan Rivers story.

"I'm not sure it was him," said Sy squirming.

"You told me he talked to you."

"He waved. Some guy playing blackjack waved to me," Sy said. "What's that prove?"

The lumpy woman frowned at the frail man, then turned to me, and said, "He saw that schoolteacher today, the one who missed the bus."

I played that line again in my head, and I knew I'd heard it right, but I just got stupid. Sy stood blinking behind his bottle-bottom lenses and my brain locked. I couldn't decide if this was the wildest stroke of luck, or an enormous pain in the ass, but I could feel a crimp developing in my dinner plans. The damn case was refusing to die a graceful death.

"You saw this guy?" I said, holding the frayed photo about six inches from the old man's nose.

"He was at the Nugget," Sy said, warming to the tale. "At a five-dollar blackjack table. He always plays low stakes in the afternoon. Says he can tell what his luck is going to be like later in the day. If he doesn't get a good feeling, he'll go to dinner, maybe see a show."

"How was he feeling?"

"I don't know, but he looked kinda beat," Sy said sadly. "He *did* have a big stack of chips in front of him though."

I struggled to frame another relevant question, but I was drawing blanks. Terry stepped from the lobby with a bucketful of keys and began making room assignments as the group reformed at the side of the bus. I thanked Sy for the tip but stopped short of telling him he did the right thing. He seemed to feel guilty about ratting Gardner out, and I let him stew. What did I know from right or wrong? I'm no philosopher. What I *did* know is that I'd soon be on my way back up the beach.

FOURTEEN

I Want to See the Bright Lights Tonight

The right thing. What was that? Was I supposed to follow this guy to the ends of the earth like in some overwrought opera? Was I adhering to some unwritten private detectives' code? Listening to my little man? Avenging some injustice? Truth to tell, I was tuning in to my own private siren song. The camcorders had come back, and they were dancing again, this time in one of those Vegas-style chorus lines, ala Merrie Melodies. Cute little camcorders with all the latest features and these long show-girl legs, high-stepping and drawing back a curtain to reveal . . . a fully equipped surveillance van! With privacy glass, car phone, and mini fridge! Look out, Sin City, here I come! I stashed my bag in my oddly adorned guest room—orange-flowered drapes, burnt sienna bedspread, orange and yellow shag carpet—then splashed my face, and hopped a cab back to America's Playground.

Cab companies charged a flat rate into town. We avoided all the construction sites, and the ride took only fifteen minutes. The city looked less seedy as the sun descended. The glow from all that neon softened the grime, and expressions on people's faces were swathed in shadow. The cab pulled past the double-parked limos to the Nugget's main entrance, and the driver asked if I was looking for some action.

"I'm just going to check out the casino," I replied naïvely.

"If you want to party later, just call this number and ask for 'Ramon,'" he said and handed me a business card with my change. The card was blank except for the phone number.

Not a shy town, Atlantic City. I thanked the driver and tipped him a buck and then stashed the card in my shirt, though I thought I'd have a hard time listing that particular service on my expense account.

The uniformed doorman was also polite, but in a chop-licking sort of way. He wanted to know if I was staying with them that night. I told him I wasn't sure yet and he let me in anyway. What a guy! Ding, ding, ding. Just like that I'd been admitted to the Magic Kingdom—no password, no secret handshake, no sign on my forehead. The price of admission was simply the willingness to put oneself in harm's way. Hop aboard and let the Seven Deadly Sins do their work. The Seven Deadly Sins and one devious designer. Once inside you were meant to stay there, until your money ran out and your credit was exhausted. Every effort had been made to create a completely self-contained, and self-absorbed, environment. Wander around and you'd find everything you needed to be happy—shops, restaurants, shows, and cash machines. Naturally, the shops only sold things you could use in the kingdom, like clothes and jewelry. Nothing that made any reference to the outside world—no newspapers, maps, or guidebooks. You could feel the Disney principles of crowd control at work, but I tried not to fight it this time. I went with the flow and—surprise, surprise—all currents flowed to the casino floor.

I had to admit there was a certain buzz in being amid all that madness, an elevating energy that made me feel a little light-headed and disoriented. I merged with the stream of sharp-eyed, sunken people that wound its way through the closely moni-tored chaos. The odds were an insult to anyone's intelligence, yet people fought one another to throw their money away, each convinced that he was more special than the next guy. The Me Generation had found a home. All these sagging sharpies were still doing The Hustle. And Billy Gardner was out there, or had been.

Bewildered, I stopped to watch some blackjack action. I couldn't find a five-dollar table, but Sy had warned me that the ante went up once the sun went down. Ten dollars was now the minimum, and there still was no shortage of takers, because on the casino floor, if you weren't playing, you weren't there. "Players" sat perched on high stools crowded around the outer edge of a crescent moon of green felt. A demurely dressed dealer—only the sauce slingers showed their tits—stood at the center and quietly slid cards. Slip, slip, slip. Cash disappeared down a plastic chute. Chips clicked and stacks shrank. No one spoke. And this was having fun? I still had my coupon quarters, so I decided to see for myself. I fed the entire roll to the same slot machine, one pull at a time. Eight coins passed through to the payoff tray. I was a winner! I stopped at a roulette table and played five dollars on twenty-seven black, but the bouncing ball refused to follow my lead. I stopped playing when I ran out of other people's money. I felt agitated, but not quite exhilarated, and *not* tempted to continue.

Maybe I was just too cheap, or chicken, to be a gambler. Simply not high stakes material. Or maybe the fun came later, for Phil was right about the working girls, those glow-in-the-dark, Black-Velvet blondes conspicuously paired with much older men. Hard to miss, the young women smiled steadily and listened more closely than any wife would. I could easily wash up on those rocks. And it wasn't hard to spot the working guys either, the beefy suits who scanned the action, who made notes and sometimes asked questions of nerdy types who sat at computer terminals in the pits and tracked play. And above all, the shiny eye in the sky, the paranoid's dream come true—someone really is watching everything you do. Once around the dance floor, I got past the people and realized the gaming layout wasn't as haphazard as it seemed. Slots had a separate section with the feel of a pinball arcade for adults. There was a horseshoe circuit of blackjack tables which started with low stakes at either end leading to big bucks in the bulging middle. Craps, roulette, and other table games occupied the infield.

Now that I had my sea legs, it was time to go to work. I fought the flow of traffic, hunkered in the eddies around each table, and scanned every blackjack face in the room. Took me two hours. Players came and went, and I couldn't stop them so I'm sure I missed a few, and after a while, more than a few got to be familiar. Or maybe it became the same face. The darting eyes edged with desperation, the tight lips and fidgety fingers, the obvious effort to appear nonchalant despite the mounting losses. The inevitable shoulder slump and eventual retreat. This had been the longest of shots, and it wasn't paying off. Some washed-out card sharp had waved to a half-blind old man, and now I was trying to sort my way through a haystack. I was feeling lost and lonely and wondered what I was missing back in Pittsburgh. I decided to take a break.

I found a lounge which overlooked the infield and slumped into a club chair at a low table along the rail. An aging beauty with crowded bosom and crusting makeup brought me a beer, for which I paid dearly since I didn't have a handle in my hand. Sleuthing was thirsty work, and the suds went down easy. Before long I was ordering another, and the waitress was looking younger, and I was feeling better about my day's work. I hadn't found my needle, but the effort had been there, and I wouldn't have any apologizing to do. I was starting to wonder if it was too late to hook up with Terry when a minor commotion broke out on the casino floor around a craps table. I passed on another round and stepped down to see what the fuss was all about.

Craps was something I hadn't checked too closely. Lots of ethnic types from the old school smoking cigars. Traditionalists. Who else could understand the game, or the betting schemes? Hard this, soft that—over, under, sideways, down. And yet it was the most interactive game on the floor. Players rolled the dice themselves, and boisterous outbursts of enthusiasm were tolerated, even encouraged, for they heralded the presence of a winner. Somebody was on a roll. A successful shooter becomes the center of the universe for the duration of his roll. The game moves to his rhythm. Tablemates catch the whiff of a winner and hop on board. A roll might not last long, but time is relative, and while it lasts—top of the world, ma! I joined the gathering crowd and watched as an average-looking, middle-aged man shook the dice and tossed them toward the opposite end of the table. The spotted cubes bounced against the padded backsplash and came to rest on the hard green felt. A chorus of cheers erupted from the crowd. Bets were paid, backs were slapped, and escorts jiggled with delight. A new round of bets was laid, and the dice were returned to the shooter. The reigning Roll Meister surveyed his subjects with a broad smile and bright eyes. He lovingly massaged the red dice and savored the moment. He could have been a lot of things in real life—an accountant, a salesman, an insurance adjustor—but here he was king. He took his time, and his subjects waited patiently. He rolled the dice between his palms, then shifted both cubes to his right hand, and shook them with an audible clatter. All eyes turned to the king as he leaned out over the table to release the dice.

I said he could have been a lot of things, but he wasn't. As the king's eyes followed the cubes, *my* eyes fixed on his face, and I realized he could only be one thing—a wayward schoolteacher from suburban Pittsburgh. I fished the crumpled snapshot from my pocket and checked the face and then checked again as another round of cheers broke out and the shooter's stack of chips continued to grow. Lady Luck had called William Gardner to the craps table where he was feeling pretty good. I wasn't feeling too bad myself. I'd found my missing man! Who cared if dumb luck had dumped him in my lap? Who had to know? I just wanted to clap Billy Boy on the back and buy him a beer, but I couldn't work my way through the crowd, so I continued to watch. More cheers and more chips, and then a murmur of apprehension rippled through the throng. Gardner had pushed the bulk of his bankroll forward, and the pit boss was questioning the bet.

"I thought this putz knew how to play," said an old codger at my elbow.

"He knows how to throw money away," replied the old guy's companion.

"He's losing it," said the first guy. "Fifty thou' on a hard eight. He's getting greedy, or stupid."

"Or both," said his friend. "Even his tootsie turned up her nose."

And, indeed, the face of the blonde at Gardner's side was clouded with concern, but the pit boss confirmed the shooter's intention and let the bet stand. Gardner rolled once, and there was more murmuring, but not much activity on the table. He rolled again and a few smiles could be seen, and a few people placed bets. Words of encouragement accompanied Gardner's third roll, but when the dice came to rest, an anguished sigh escaped from the crowd. Gardner slumped at the rail, and the betting grid was cleared. The shooter's stack of chips was a fraction of what it had been. The deflated audience drifted away, and the stickman tried to entice a new shooter. I waited till Gardner raised his head and then made my way to the table.

"William Gardner, I presume," I said glibly when I'd reached the shooter's side, too delighted with my fortuitous find to take stock of the schoolteacher's shell-shocked condition. And yet, when Busted Billy turned to me, I could scarcely ignore the change in his appearance. His eyes had gone glassy, his cheeks were sunken, and his complexion had taken on the waxy sheen of a cadaver. I looked toward the Black-Velvet blonde and saw a young woman who'd run away from a small town to become a porn star. No more fun house reflections. I blinked twice and tried again.

"Hey, man, I've been looking for you. You've got everybody back home all worked up," I said, obstinately obtuse as Gardner stared back blankly. "Listen, dude, I'm a private investigator from Pittsburgh. You remember Pittsburgh, right? Your wife hired me to find your sorry ass and I've got a few offers I'd like to discuss." Still no response. "Hel-lo! You look like you could use a drink. How 'bout I buy you a beer?"

Zippo. Gardner turned back to the table, caught the eye of a stocky suit in the pit area, and then proceeded to load his remaining chips into a plastic rack.

"Hey, tag, you're it, pal," I said, placing my hand on his arm which caused him to fumble a few chips. "I found you fair and square. Five minutes is all I'm asking."

What I got was a demonstration on how the house removes unruly elements from the gaming area. Two low-profile bouncers emerged from the dwindling crowd. Each grabbed an arm, my arms, and twisted in such a way as to keep me upright and moving toward a door marked, "Security." Gardner never said a word. When I looked back over my shoulder, I saw that he had resumed racking his chips.

"Excuse me, can I have my arms back?" I asked the two goons as we proceeded down a hallway on the far side of the Security door.

No reply as we rounded a corner and headed toward another door which opened onto a deserted loading dock. The two toughs stopped at the edge of the dock and then launched me in the general direction of an empty trash dumpster. Fortunately, I fell short and landed in a stack of cardboard boxes which had been used to transport fresh fruit and vegetables. Lucky me. As I lay there taking inventory, I heard the house hoods chuckle to themselves, and then the door closed, and I was alone.

FIFTEEN

Everybody Knows This Is Nowhere

The toe bone's connected to the foot bone, and the foot bone's connected to the ankle bone, and the ankle bone's connected to the shin bone, now, hear the word of the Lord!

Only after I determined that I was physically alright did I take the time to get seriously irritated, still refusing to accept that my timing, and approach, were terribly off. The guy had just lost fifty thousand dollars, and I was the one who felt aggrieved. Party on, Frank.

"Fucking-A, man!" I shouted to the black sky and blank walls. Whatever happened to playing by the rules? Hell, the only rule in this town was whatever you could get away with, and if you were losing big bucks in a casino, you could get away with practically anything. Line up the seven deadly sins and take your pick. But I wasn't about to give up on my bonuses that easy. I emerged from the box pile reeking of cantaloupe with little bits of green decay clinging to my clothes. I found my way to a side street and then followed the building around to the main hotel entrance on Pacific Avenue. The doorman wasn't too thrilled to see me this time, but I didn't stop to chat and opened the door myself. I marched straight to the front desk and asked for William Gardner.

"Is he a guest of the hotel, sir?" asked the uniformed clerk; "Christine" according to her name tag.

"Yes, he's a guest of the goddam hotel."

"Would you happen to know what room he's in?" asked Christine.

"If I knew what room he was in, I'd be on my way up there."

"I'm sorry sir, we don't have a William Carner registered," she said, demonstrating just how much of a pain in the ass *she* was prepared to be.

"*Gardner,* with a 'g' and a 'd,'" I emphasized snottily.

"We don't have one of those either," the clerk said without looking. "Perhaps you'd like to check at our Security Desk?" she added sweetly.

I didn't think it would help my case much to explain that I'd just been tossed by Security, but I didn't have much choice, so I reluctantly headed in that direction, hoping I wouldn't run into the same no-necks who'd given me the bum's rush. Thankfully, this time the security guys were older and wore gray suits. The first two had been younger and wore black suits. This was supposed to be a playground, and it was choked with guys in suits. I pleaded my case, and they checked my ID, but they were less than sympathetic and not inclined to help, so I decided to bail and try my luck at another entrance. I went out, took a short stroll, and tried to re-enter three doors down, but the eye in the sky was working overtime. Three steps in I was intercepted by two double-wide guards wearing uniforms, sidearms, and nasty expressions. The jig was up, and I knew it. I went without a fuss. Two local boys in blue collected me at the curb and promised a short trip to a long night in the city lock-up. I was too annoyed with myself to respond, but they must have been bored, or out of doughnuts, because they asked me what I'd done to deserve the untimely eviction. I was too embarrassed to tell the truth, so I started spinning some half-assed tale about my father squandering his retirement fund at the gaming tables and leaving my mother penniless. I don't think they believed me, but I was wearing my tie and looking pathetic, so they warned me away from the Nugget and asked if I had a place to stay. They knew the Shifting Sands, but it was off their turf, so they just dropped me at the edge of town and pointed me south.

"Just keep walking, kid," was their advice as I stood blinking stupid on the sidewalk; then they made an abrupt U-turn on the broad avenue and headed back to the bright lights.

I didn't even think of following. Obviously, there were people a lot more serious about this shit than I was, and I'd met a few too many of them already tonight. Let the asshole stay lost if that's what he wanted. How could I even be sure it was him? I summoned what was left of my self-respect and started walking. Along the beach at first, but it was way dark down there, and I got sand in my shoes. Then on the Boardwalk, which in that area was essentially a double-wide residential sidewalk that just happened to be made of rainforest hardwood raised above replenished shoreline. A mix of apartments, condos, and mansions faced the water, but all their windows were dark, and I started to worry about getting mugged. I started thinking that I could get hit on the head and forget who I was and wake up in the Frank Sinatra Wing without my wallet. I wondered how long it would take before someone came looking for *me*. And I thought, if they hired someone like me to look, I could be lost a long time. So, I trudged back to Atlantic Avenue where there wasn't much traffic, and nobody out strolling the streets, but at least I wasn't balanced on the edge of the abyss. Like, if I got hit on the head, I'd still remember who I was. None of which made any sense, so I started thinking the real problem was I hadn't had much to eat all day, and yet I walked all the way back to the motel, about fifty blocks, without seeing as much as a sandwich shop.

I was in sad shape when I stopped in the lobby to ask a different desk clerk where a guy could get a bite to eat. He looked worried as hell seeing me all rumpled and stinky until I showed him my room key and told him I'd gotten mugged. Another story to salvage some self-respect. The clerk showed some sympathy and then directed me to a sub shop a block over, but I decided to clean up first before I worried anyone else. I stopped in my room, picked all the green debris out of my hair and off my clothes, and then washed and combed myself till I looked presentable. There wasn't much I could do about the cantaloupe cologne. I found Dino's Deli, where the desk clerk said it would be, and ordered a Philly-style cheese steak and a six-pack of Rolling Rock to go. I planned to spend the rest of the night in my room, getting buzzed, watching something stupid on TV. Terry would have to find someone else to buy her a drink, like that'd be a problem. I thought about giving somebody back home a call, but Trudy might still be in date mode, and Des would either be asleep or making a fool of himself at Rodolfo's, demanding to see "the

tapes." I thought maybe my client would like to know her meat-
head husband was still alive, but I figured that could wait till
morning. *You're on your own, kid*, I said to myself as I walked
back huffing the fried-onion, grilled-steak, gooey-cheese fumes.
And yet I wasn't feeling bad about that, being on my own. I'd
learned a few things about myself, and I'd made enough money
to pay the rent. The bonuses were not meant to be, but I might yet
get a date with the tour leader. So, all in all, I was feeling pretty
good, till I opened the door to my room and found a man with a
gun in my bed.

"Come all the way in," said the pallid intruder with a wave of
his hardware. "Close the door behind you."

"What the fuck—,"

"Step in and close the door!" he repeated with some urgency.

"Gardner?" I wondered in disbelief.

"Hey, tag, you're it, pal," he said, wearily mocking me.

"Sonuvabitch! It really is you," I said as I stepped into the
room, with some trepidation, and confronted the sunken schoolteacher for the second time that night. I suppose I should have
been glad to find my man again, but I really don't like guns.

"Close the door," he said. "Anybody with you out there?"

"Just me," I said as I closed the door behind me.

"What's in the bag?"

"My dinner. Cheesesteak and a six-pack."

"Sit down," he said with a gracious wave of his gun. "We'll
have a drink together."

A small table and two chairs were set up where a second bed might have been. I placed the bag on the table, pulled the six-pack out, and worked two cans free from their plastic rings. Gardner had been watching TV. He had a small pistol in one hand and the TV remote in the other. He used the remote to lower the sound and then dropped it as I handed him an opened Rolling Rock. His hand shook as he reached for the can, but he held the gun steady enough. I sat in the straight-backed chair that faced the bed and opened my beer. My dinner would have to wait.

"Now, who sent you?" he said as he took a swig from his Rock.

"Excuse me," I said, still struggling to comprehend. "Could you lower that gun just a little? Trust me, I'm not the heroic type."

"Don't fuck with me, kid," he said shaking his gat before letting it come to rest on the bed beside him. "Who sent you?"

"Take your pick," I said and shrugged, trying to act nonchalant. "Your wife, her girlfriend, your mother-in-law?"

"What are you, some sort of private cop?"

"Something like that. Detective, investigator, whatever. From Pittsburgh."

"You're not with that Wheaton whacko, then?"

"Who's Wheaton?" I said, but he waved the question away and stared at the murmuring TV.

Billy Boy looked fried. He also looked like he'd been mixing something edgy with his alcohol. He was struggling to focus his attention, but too many things seemed to weigh on what little mind he had left. I thought if I waited long enough, he might just drift off, but then I thought about the bonus money. And the camcorders were dusting off their dancing shoes, so I decided to try and reel the spaceman in. Ground control to Major Bill. Can you hear me, Major Bill?

"You alright, dude?" I asked. "Something I can help you with?"

"I'll be fine," he said, though I personally wasn't convinced. "We're just going to wait here a while," he said, then smiled cheerlessly, and sipped his beer.

"How did you find me?" I asked out of professional curiosity since I was the one who was supposed to do the finding.

"Followed the breadcrumbs," he said.

"Breadcrumbs?"

"You told that second set of security guards where you were staying, ya dope."

"And they just passed that on to you?"

"I'd just lost a lot of money," he said and seemed sapped by the memory. "Those places take care of their big losers."

"But how'd you get in the room?"

"Pretty embarrassing to get caught with your pants down, eh, kid?" he said with a chuckle and then sipped his beer before continuing. "I took a cab down. Told the desk clerk I was rooming with you, and he just gave me a key. Said you'd just stepped out for something to eat."

I had to admit; it was pretty embarrassing to be hoisted by my own petard. Caught short by someone with a penchant for making shit up. "Just what are we waiting for?" I asked.

"Say what?"

"You said we were going to wait a while. What are we waiting for?"

"For the coast to be clear," he said with some irritation, so I let it drop.

"Why'd you come looking for *me*?" I asked. "Ready to head home."

"I wasn't looking for you. I was just looking for a place to lay low."

"Thought Big Red might be waiting for you?" I said with a smirk.

He looked at me suspiciously for a moment and then smiled himself. "So you really are a detective, huh?" He thought a moment and shook his head before continuing. "Big Red. She doesn't even know my name. I was feeling goofy one night and sent out a bunch of postcards."

"You sent one to Ann Deaver too."

"Yeah, I guess I did."

"She's worried about you."

"Annie's been worried about me for years. Me and my potential," he said and then went back to staring at the TV.

I was almost starting to feel sorry for the guy. Except for the fact that he was holding me hostage, he didn't seem like a total jerk. "So why'd you run away?" I asked, trying to get his train back on track. "Couldn't handle the whole 'daddy' deal?"

"What 'daddy' deal?" he said, snapping out of his funk and raising his weapon. "I thought you didn't know him?"

"Know who?"

"Harold Wheaton. The bimbo's father."

"What bimbo?"

"From the casino."

"The blonde with the big boobs?"

"Christ! She look sixteen to you? I never seen a rack like that on a teenager."

"Her father's after you?"

"Guy's my age," he said and shook his head, oblivious to what that said about *him*. "He threatened to cut my balls off!"

"So, you got yourself a gun," I said, which had to be illegal, this being New Jersey, which, unlike Pennsylvania, had some strict gun laws.

"He showed up at the casino right after you," he said, implying that Harold and I were in cahoots, and not commenting on the provenance of his firearm. "He made a scene, so I split."

"I never met the guy," I said, "And I only saw the girl that once."

He still looked suspicious, but at least he'd stopped waving the pistol around. He drained his Rock, crumpled the can, and tossed it in a corner. "How 'bout another beer?" he said.

I pulled another can loose, popped the top, and handed it over. "Why'd you run away from *Pittsburgh*?" I asked after he'd settled a bit.

"Say what?"

"Pittsburgh, remember? Fox Hollow? You had a pretty nice setup back there. Why'd you run away?"

"Fuck you. I didn't run away. I took the bus down," he said with a sneer that sent me back to thinking he *was* an asshole. "I was riding a roll. I was up a hundred thou' at one point. Maybe I lost track of time. So what? Goddam casino comps me an escort and now this looney toon wants my balls."

"What happened to the money?"

"You win some, you lose some."

"You lost it all?"

"Lady Luck's a tramp, kid," he said. More words of wisdom from an elder.

"Man, why don't you just go home?" I asked in exasperation. I was getting really fed up with this guy.

"I've got one good run left in me," he said, oblivious, and it was apparent that common sense had long since left the building. "I was almost there tonight. This shit'll settle down."

"I must be missing something," I said shaking my head. "You're losing touch."

"Fuck you. It could happen."

"Win big? You're dreaming. You planning a remake of *Guys and Dolls* here? And suppose you do, win big. Then what?"

"Then I walk away and start over. Without all the goddam expectations."

"You could do that, just blow off your wife, your life back in the 'burbs?"

"Liz gets along without me very well," he said. "She wouldn't miss me much, and she certainly doesn't need my money."

"What about the baby? You blow that off too?" I asked with some heat, despite the gun.

"What baby?"

"Your baby! Your wife's pregnant, remember? Odds are she'll have a baby."

"Lizzie's pregnant?" he said half to himself. "You sure?"

"Man, you *are* losing touch."

"*My* wife's having a baby?" he said again. The Spaceman seemed genuinely surprised, and skeptical.

"Yes, you stupid shitheel. Your wife's having a baby."

Gardner seemed to think that was pretty funny. He spent the next minute chuckling like a madman. "Shit, she may be having a baby," he finally said, "But *I* sure as hell am not the father." More chuckles. "I took care of that years ago," he continued. "Christ, that was just one of the many things Liz and I could never agree on. She was so set on it that I started thinking she might just stop taking the pill, and not tell me, so I did what I had to do myself. Hurt like hell, but it put my mind at ease."

"You had a vasectomy? You can't have kids?" I said, squirming in my seat at the thought of what he'd had done.

"Not if I wanted to."

"Who's the father then?"

"How the hell should I know? You're the detective."

"It's gotta be somebody's baby," I said, half to myself.

"Biology major, right?" he said with a snort. "Hey, maybe I should hire you to find out? That could be worth something." And he looked for a moment like he was thinking about it. "You know, somebody could be blowing smoke up your skirt," he continued. "This sounds like one of Allie's schemes. Now, *there's* a piece of work." Wink, wink. Nudge, nudge.

Billy Boy was enjoying himself now, but he still looked like hell. I couldn't make sense of this baby business, but the train was pulling into Bonusville, so I didn't much care. "She wants to talk to you," I said.

"Who, Allie? I wanted to do more than talk, but I could never get Liz interested in a little group activity, if you know what I mean?" Still winking and nudging.

"You knew about them?"

"Allie's been sniffing around for a while now, but she's swimming upstream with Liz," he said. "Lizzie's pretty straitlaced about sex. Unlike her mother." This guy couldn't help himself.

"She wants to talk to you too," I said, trying to bring him back to my bonus.

"Fucking, Mona. Talk, talk, talk. Not like the good old days. She's shriveled up and nasty now, but you should have seen her twenty years ago."

"She's upped her offer to a quarter of a million dollars," I said, in awe of the figure, but Gardner only curled his lip. He was not impressed.

"She had quite the nice ass for an old broad, " Billy continued reminiscing.

"That must have been a while ago," I replied absently, but Wayward Will was in his element.

"Liz and I were still in college," he recalled. "I went home with her one weekend to meet the parents. Old Mona made quite a first impression." This time he literally did wink. I tried to ignore yet another implication, but Billy Boy was rolling. "She sent Liz and her father out on some half-assed errand before I got up. I come down to the kitchen and there's Mona at the sink rinsing dishes. She's got this long, loose robe on. I sit down at the table, and she offers me a cup of coffee. Sounds good to me. So, she gets the coffee and when she sets the mug down, the robe slips open, and she's got nothing on underneath. Absolutely nothing." He paused for effect. "Like I said, nice piece of ass for an old broad."

"Are you trying to tell me you made it with your mother-in-law?"

"Well, she wasn't my mother-in-law back then," he said as if it made a difference. "I think Mona had just seen *The Graduate* or something. She thought I was such a loser that Liz and I would never stay together. She's been trying to get rid of me ever since."

"For that kind of money, why not just go?"

"If I could only trust the bitch to keep her end of the bargain, I would."

I'd more than had it with this guy. Trouble was, he still had his gun, and he was starting to look comfortable. "I don't get it, man," I said, and I didn't. "What's your fucking problem? I mean, what's all the whining about? You made this mess. Nobody put a gun to *your* head. Just walk away."

"You wouldn't understand. And I'm not walking away with nothing."

"I'll tell you what I don't understand," I said, and I still didn't. "I don't understand all that crap in your room back home. The tapes, the Sierra Club, the tickets to Woodstock. You still believe in any of that shit?"

"You been poking through my stuff?" he said with a flash of annoyance, and then he sighed and turned thoughtful. "Things were different back then," was all he had to offer.

I thought I was going to puke, but then again, Crosby, Stills, and Nash had hit the casino circuit singing, "We can cha-ange the world." Maybe Billy Boy had just followed along.

"That's pretty lame," I said. "I've been hearing that my whole life." Babes got lost in the wood. Boo-hoo. But Boomer Bill's ears were stuffed with nostalgia. My missing man was still struggling to find himself, and he obviously liked where he'd been better than where he'd ended up.

"I still remember the day I bought those tickets," reminisced the Ramblin' Man with the dreamy look. "At Jerry's Records in New Brunswick. 'Three days of peace and music' sounded sweet at the time, what with the draft and all, but I couldn't get any of my lame ass friends to go with me, so I freaked my parents out and went by myself. On the bus. Got as far as Port Authority and the ticket clerk tells me the roads are closed and I won't be able to get through. So, I bailed. Got a room in a flea bag hotel, hung around Times Square for a few days, and then took the bus back. Told everybody they'd stopped collecting tickets by the time I got there. Had 'em framed and hung 'em on the wall."

"You're talking about Woodstock, right?"

"Yeah, the first one."

"Christ, they were right about you," I said with a mix of awe and aggravation. "You *are* a total sleazeball."

"Shit, listen to you talk. What the fuck're you doing with *your* life? Watching the world go by? Playing video games? Poking in other people's shit like some pervert peeping tom."

"It's a living," I said, though it sounded weak even to me. "You know, things aren't always what they seem. Hell, I never said I was out to change the world. You've been a teacher for ten years. Working with little kids. Doesn't that mean anything to you?"

"Damn kids will eat you alive. They're needy little bastards," he said as he shook his head and then thought for a moment before continuing. "I don't know. I've never been good at that shit, growing up and whatnot. But at the end of the day, you gotta look like you're doing something with your life. You can't sit on the sidelines and watch forever. Pick a song and learn to dance."

Christ almighty. He was talking in circles, chasing his tail. And if this was dancing, sitting on the sidelines might be the better way to go. I was about to ask him to name that tune—Dancing in the Dark?—when a commotion broke out in the courtyard. Major Bill may have been paranoid, but it was starting to sound like someone really was out to get him.

"I know you're in here somewhere," came an angry voice followed by a loud thumping a few rooms down.

"Over by the door," Gardner said as he sat upright and swung his feet to the floor. "When he starts pounding, you pull it open and stand clear."

"What're you gonna do?"

"Don't worry, I'll handle it," he said, but I didn't feel assured. Should I bother to remind him that we were no longer in a casino, and he wouldn't get comped for shooting someone?

Gardner stood by the bed now, preparing to face down his pursuer. I couldn't figure out how I'd been transported to the middle of an old *Gunsmoke* episode, but I wanted out of this alternate universe. Like, now.

"Listen," I said as I stood, thinking I'd offer to go out and talk to the guy, but Gardner cut me off.

"Move it," he said and waved me to the door with his six-shooter.

I started toward the door, but something snapped, and I turned back suddenly and grabbed his gun arm. I couldn't believe I'd done something that stupid. Gardner grinned like a madman, and we waltzed around the room knocking over tables and lamps. The gun went off with a loud, BANG! and I felt pain sear down my left leg. Gardner pushed me away, and I tripped over a chair leg and fell backward. I hit my head and the lights went out.

SIXTEEN

Baby, Now That I've Found You

I came to as a pair of paramedics strapped me to a stretcher. The lights seemed awfully bright, but my arms weren't free so all I could do was turn my head and blink. I hadn't noticed before how ugly the ceiling was. Water-stained tiles sagged overhead, and dead flies collected in the light fixture. I winced.

"He's coming around," said one of the paramedics.

"Where am I?" I asked, and for a moment, I really didn't know.

"New Jersey," said the paramedic with a smile.

"Shit," I said as the day's events came dribbling back.

"Where's the gun?" asked a uniformed police officer with a pleasant face and a ponytail.

"What gun?"

"A shot was fired in this room? Where's the gun?"

"I don't like guns," I said.

"We should get a move on," said the paramedic.

The officer seemed reluctant to let me go but finally nodded and said, "I'll follow you over."

With that, the paramedics lifted me over the threshold and rolled me to the back of their waiting rescue wagon. Only the worried-looking desk clerk watched as they hoisted me on board and swung the doors shut.

"How bad is it?" I asked the paramedic who rode in back with me.

"You'll live," he assured me, but I must not have looked convinced, so he followed up with some details. "You have a scalp laceration that's going to need stitches. And you have an unusual abrasion to your leg. The gun must have been pressed against your thigh when it went off. Lucky for you it was pointing down."

"Shit, I don't remember."

"You may not for a while. You've had a concussion."

I remembered coming back to my room and finding Gardner in my bed, and I remembered thinking the guy was a total douchebag, but I couldn't remember exactly why I felt that way. "Hey, you think I'll get to stay in the Frank Sinatra Wing?" I asked.

"Sorry, wrong hospital," said my attendant. "The Sinatra Wing's downtown. We're going to Shore Memorial." I frowned and he added, "You're better off on the mainland. The city's a zoo on Saturday night, and you won't be staying over anyway."

The "mainland" must have been closer too, for in just a few minutes, we were pulling up to the emergency room door. The paramedics wheeled me into an almost empty lobby where I filled out a form and left a credit card imprint since I couldn't prove I had health insurance. Couldn't prove it 'cause I didn't have it. Another item for my expense report. At length I was parked in an examination room with a large window looking out onto the main ER triage area where the woman in blue who had followed us over conferred with a woman in white who turned out to be an ER doctor. A nurse entered the room and went about confirming the information compiled by the paramedics after which she left to confer with the doctor.

Hel-lo-o! In here, doc! Let me introduce myself. I'm *the patient*. Without me, you've got no reason to confer. I was beginning to lose mine. Patience, that is, but finally the Big Kahuna made her entrance, flashed me a frigid, "I'm-a-doctor-and-you're-not" smile, and asked insincerely, "How we doing in here?"

"My head hurts," I said, but she ignored me and scanned my chart. "My leg too."

"Is your vision blurred at all?" she asked while shining a pen light in my eyes.

"No."

"Any nausea or dizziness?" she asked, looking first at my leg and then the back of my head.

"Nope," I said again.

"The nurse will clean you up and get you ready," she announced cheerily. "I'll be back in a few minutes to stitch your head." And with that she was gone. Off to confer with who knows who about who knows what. Ah, the joys of managed health care. As in, how fast can I *manage* to stitch this slob up so I can get back to the more important things in life, like *managing* my stock portfolio, and choosing a color for the interior of my new Mercedes.

Thankfully, the nurse was good at what she did, though she seemed to be sleepwalking while she was doing it. Then again, it was the middle of the night. She cleaned my leg and closed the gash with a few butterflies before wrapping it up. Then she helped me move to this crazy chair with arm rests, a straight, high back, and a chin rest which swung in from the side. She cleaned the back of my head and carefully shaved around the wound, at which point, the lady doctor returned with Officer Ponytail in tow. Ms. Bedside Manner applied a local anesthetic and then proceeded with her repair work.

"You remember yet what happened to the gun?" asked the officer, but this time, I was ready for her. I'd love it if they picked up Gardner, but I wasn't giving anybody any reason to fall in love with me. As a suspect, that is. In other words, my head was clear enough to sling some shit.

"I came down from Pittsburgh on one of those bus tours," I said. "I crapped out at the casino, so I went back to the motel before the rest of the group. I got some take-out from a sub shop. On my way back to my room, this guy with a gun grabs me and tells me he needs a place to hide out for a while. Who am I to argue? We go to my room and drink a few beers while we're watching TV. He hears some commotion in the courtyard, and he gets up to check it out. I make a grab for the gun, and it goes off. Then I fell and hit my head, and that's when the lights went out."

"Who was this guy?"

"Don't know."

"You never saw him before?"

"Not that I remember," I said and then asked, "You catch him?" But she ignored me.

Apparently, Officer Ponytail hadn't gotten much help from anyone else, or she would have pushed me harder. As it was, she didn't have much to go on. I was the one with the bloody head and leg. The gun was gone, and I'd been knocked unconscious. How could I be a suspect? For once, I wasn't trying to be a pain in the ass, just more trouble than I was worth, and I seemed to be succeeding.

"Will he be alright to travel?" the officer asked the doctor.

"We'll give him a list of 'dos and don'ts,'" the doctor said. "As long as someone's with him, he's good to go."

"I'll be on the bus," I offered helpfully, but just then an agitated, middle-aged stranger appeared outside the room and peered in at me. "Who's that?" I asked.

"You ever see *him* before?" asked the officer.

"Not that I remember," I said, and I wasn't lying.

"He could have some gaps," said the doctor.

"Guy lost his daughter," said the officer. "He's a little distraught."

"She died?"

"Ran away."

"That's a shame," I said, and with that, the guy turned abruptly and walked toward the exit.

"He's all set," said the doctor, and after stopping at the admissions desk, I was on my way.

Officer Ponytail offered me a ride back to the motel, and I offered to take her out to breakfast, which she thought was pretty funny. She suggested I clean myself up and change my clothes before I went anywhere. "You smell like cantaloupe," she said, then she gave me her card, and asked me to call if I remembered anything.

And so there I was, back at the scene of the crime, standing uncertainly on the sidewalk in front of the Shifting Sands. The sky had begun to lighten, but the sun wasn't up yet, and the motel's neon sign buzzed above me. I saw a laundry cart stacked with fresh sheets, but I didn't see the maid around, and I was thankful for the chance to sneak back in. My room smelled sourly of spent gunpowder, but there were fried onions on the air as well and I remembered how hungry I was. I also remembered why I thought Gardner was such an asshole. The room was still a mess, but my sub-shop bag was still on the table, and I crossed the room in eager anticipation. Alas, the bag was empty.

"Sorry, I'm eating your cheesesteak," came a voice from behind me, and I almost peed my pants. I wheeled round to find the distraught dad from the hospital sitting in the corner of the room. He had a gun in one hand and my sub in the other. Yet another gun. In New Jersey no less. And how were all these looney tunes getting loose in my room? I didn't even want to know anymore, but, apparently, this motel had a rather liberal open-door policy.

"Christ, it's like the Wild West around here," I said, trying to summon some attitude. "Everybody's got a gun."

"No need to be taking the Lord's name in vain," said the man in the corner with the gun. He sounded serious. As in, he wasn't joking about the Lord's name. "I'll pay you for the cheesesteak."

"Who the hell are *you*?"

"Harold Wheaton."

"The bimbo's father?"

"She's not a bimbo, and I'm not her father," he said as angrily as he could with a mouthful of my sub.

"Sorry, I've had a long night," I said. I have a real knack for making first impressions.

"Where is he?" he asked.

"Where's who?" I replied hoping we weren't starting another round of *Who's On First?*

"That fancy-pants gambling man who was in here last night."

"You should know better than me. You were waiting for him right outside the door. How'd he get away?"

"He had a gun," he said somewhat sheepishly. "Mine was in my truck. Sonuvabitch jumped the bulkhead and I lost him."

"Well, if I knew where he was, I'd be there myself. Or the police would," I said, wearily patting the bandage on the back of my head. "I've got a score to settle."

"If you don't know where he went, you know who he is."

"I never saw him before he broke in here last night," I said, trying to distance myself from the fugitive philanderer.

"The maid said you've been showing his picture around," Harold said as he set the sub aside. "Now, you're gonna help me find him, and he's gonna do the right thing."

"About what?"

"Tiffany, and her child. She's pregnant and he's the one who did it."

Christ, not another baby. "If she's not your daughter, why do you care?"

"That's no concern of yours," he said shaking his head. "I've been taking care of that girl for most of her life." I started to think about it but stopped myself. I didn't want to go down some winding, backwoods lane to find a slumping shack nestled in a clearing and have some woodchuck like Karl Malden or Buddy Ebsen answer the door while little Tiffany cowered in the background. Harold was right. It was no concern of mine. My main worry was how to get this simple-minded nutcase out of my room before his gun went off and I got grazed again. Or worse.

"Mind if I sit down?" I asked as I stooped to pick up a chair. Harold didn't object so I sat. Things were getting too complicated. It was time to get back to basics, all the way back to the birds and the bees. "Listen, your Tiffany and this guy were only together for a week, right? How could she know she's pregnant already?"

"This was not the first time. She told me."

"Harold, I happen to know this guy is not capable of fathering a child. Physically, I mean."

"So, you do know him."

"He's a schoolteacher from Pittsburgh," I said with a sigh. "His wife hired me to find him."

"Well, I don't expect him to marry her," Harold said reasonably. "But he *will* do right by that child. Money-wise."

"You're a little late for that, aren't you? He lost all that money back to the casino."

"The family's got money. Tiff told me."

"His *wife's* got money, and *she* wants a divorce. She'll be only too happy to hear about this little escapade."

"Don't think you're gonna talk your way out of this," he said as he stood. "We're leaving right now."

"Leaving for where?"

"Pittsburgh."

"What, you're gonna ride back on the bus holding me at gun point?" No way Terry was letting this madman *near* the bus.

"My truck's outside. We'll drive. Now, move it," he said with a wave of his gun.

The thought of riding six hours in a pick-up with this fruit loop was more than I could bear. He'd want me to drive while he kicked back, chewing tobacco, snacking on Slim Jims, listening to Garth Brooks and Wynonna. And yet, there was no leap left in my legs, and I wasn't about to go waltzing with another sleep-deprived whacko.

"Let me just get my things together," I said, but as I got up, there was a soft tap on the door.

"Don't move," he hissed and waved me back.

"Harold, I know you're in there," came a young woman's voice and louder knock.

"Baby?" said Harold as he moved to open the door, and there stood the voluptuous blond casino escort, looking much more like the high school student she should have been.

"Oh, Daddy, put that thing away," she said referring to the gun as she breezed into the room. Harold closed the door and put the pistol in his pocket.

"You shouldn't be here, Tiff," said Harold. "I told you I'd take care of this. That man's gonna do right by you."

"I'm not pregnant, Daddy," she said with a sigh. "So you can leave that man alone."

"But you said . . . and that he was the one."

"I was mad because you came after me, but you're taking this too far," she said in a bit of an understatement. "I've got to live my own life now, Harold. I can't stay with you forever."

"But you need someone to take care of you."

"I'm old enough to take care of myself," she said, though it hardly seemed possible. "That's the way it'll have to be."

Harold slumped into his chair and buried his face in his hands. Tiffany laid her hand affectionately on his shoulder and then turned to me and asked, "What the heck happened to you?"

"I fell," I said and smiled.

"Harold didn't do that, did he?" she asked with some concern.

"No, the high-roller was here."

"Mr. Gardner did that?"

"You knew his name?" I asked, a little surprised.

She nodded. "I didn't tell Harold because I was afraid of what he might do."

"When did you see him last?"

"At the casino last night. Right after you got thrown out, Harold showed up and made a total scene. I just split and spent the night with a friend."

"You have no idea where he might have gone?"

"Not if he didn't go back to the casino."

"He ever talk about anyone, or say anything that might give you an idea?" I asked grasping at straws.

"God, we didn't talk much," she said with a shy smile, and I could see Harold shake his head. "We watched old movies, he liked to watch me strip to music like I was working in some club. And he'd take long walks on the Boardwalk by himself." She paused and I gave her room. "He was a nice enough guy," she continued, "But he seemed to think winning all that money was gonna make a big difference, like it meant something. He woke up the next day, and he was still the same person." She shook her head. "Then his luck changed, and he couldn't walk away. Strictly a streak shooter."

She seemed like a nice kid, and I was tempted to give her a lecture about her line of work, but I knew she wouldn't listen. I know I wouldn't have listened when I was her age. Hell, I *still* wasn't paying much attention. "If by some chance he does get in touch with you, just give me a call, okay?" I said and found her one of my business cards that wasn't smudged with taco sauce.

"Sure," she said, taking the card. "There's no need to be calling the police now, is there?"

"No," I said. "Just be careful out there."

Tiffany smiled and turned to her deflated guardian. "C'mon, Daddy," she said softly and then guided the still-miserable man into the morning light.

SEVENTEEN

Bringing It All Back Home

I listened for the sound of Harold's departing pickup, then set the security chain, and sat back heavily on the bed, wincing in pain. Whatever they had given me at the hospital was wearing off. I seemed to remember packing some Extra-Strength Tylenol, but I couldn't remember where. As I sat and summoned strength for the search, a knock came at the door. More fucking company was the last thing I wanted just then, and I was way past being polite.

"Go away," I shouted, or tried to shout. The best I could manage was an angry croak.

"Frank, it's me, Terry," came the sweet-sounding reply, and suddenly having company didn't seem like such a bad idea.

"Just a sec," I called, but as I swung my feet to the floor, I was slowed by a rush of pain and nausea. I staggered to the door, slipped the security chain, and opened up to my tempting tour leader, clad in sweat suit and sneakers, looking deliciously dewy.

"Oh, my god, Frank!" she said as she crossed the threshold. "What happened to you?" But before I could reply, she spied a brownish stain on the orange shag carpet. "Oh, my god! Is that blood? Is that *your* blood?"

"Yeah, I guess so," I said, noticing the stain for the first time.

"Christ, Frank, this place is a mess," she said after surveying the damage. "You'll have to pay for this." Nothing like a little sympathy for the detective to take the edge off a long night.

"I'm fine, thanks," I said, closing the door and then gimping across the room for effect. "Just a little flesh wound and a bump on the head. What's a little brain damage between friends?"

"Oh, I'm sorry. Are you alright?" she asked, sounding concerned, but then she looked around again at the disheveled room. "Jeez, Frank, I was going to offer some help, but if you're in trouble, forget it."

"Take it easy, old girl. I'm not in any trouble, and this has nothing to do with you," I said. "Take a load off and lighten up."

Terry sat on the edge of the chair next to the little table and folded her hands in her lap. I sat back on the bed and winced. "Can I get you anything?" she asked and I thought if I gave her something to do, it might take her mind off the mess.

"I think there's some Tylenol in my shaving kit, in the bathroom," I said. "Can you get me a couple?"

Terry went into the bathroom and came back with two pills and a glass of water. I thanked her and swallowed the pills. She waited for the glass which she set on the table as she retook her seat. "So what happened, Frank?" she said again as she settled.

"It's a long story. I'm getting there," I assured her, but first there were a few things *I* needed to know. "What time you guys get back last night?"

"I'm not sure. I think it was around two. We got back just as the ambulance was pulling out."

"You see anybody suspicious hanging around?"

"The police were here. They wouldn't let us off the bus right away. They said there'd been a robbery, and they wanted to check all the rooms first."

"They catch anybody?"

"Not that I know of."

"Well, I'm the guy who got robbed," I said, deciding to keep things on a need-to-know basis.

"You were in the ambulance?"

"That was me."

"God, what did you have worth stealing?"

"Well, the guy didn't actually take anything. He was kinda strung out. He had a gun; I tried to take it away. It went off and I fell and hit my head."

"Jesus, Frank, it's only money," she said. "It's not worth getting shot for." So much for the sympathy.

"I'll remember that next time," I said. "But if it was money he'd been looking for, I would have given it to him. He was acting a little crazy and I was afraid what he might do."

"Sheesh," was all she had to offer, and we sat awkwardly for a moment. "Sy said he saw that schoolteacher," she said at length.

"Yeah, he told me too."

She thought for another moment and then apparently decided she didn't want to know the answer to whatever question she was about to ask. "Christ, Frank," she said instead with a curl of her luscious lip, "You can't go home on the bus like that."

"I have some clean clothes, but I'll need help changing. If you could just pull my pants off for me," I said suggestively.

"In your dreams," she said as she stood up. "If you really need help, I'll ask Earl to stop by. I have to check on the coffee and danish."

"Drop by any time," I called as she closed the door behind her. And what a lovely behind it was, definitely worth a dream or two. And I could have started right away. I did, in fact, lay back for a minute, but before I could peel those sweatpants off my dream girl, a horn sounded through the fog in my brain, and I prodded myself upright. No time for a nap, Frank.

I needed a plan, but I was having trouble stringing two thoughts together. I decided a splash of water might sharpen my focus, so I made my way to the bathroom and discovered why Terry had been in such a rush to get out. I looked like hell. Scary even, with spiked hair, sunken eyes, and bloodstained shirt collar. Not to mention the pants leg which was slit to the crotch exposing my underwear—briefs, which were now stained with Betadine. I felt like running out myself, but I had nowhere to go, so I stuck around and cleaned up the best I could.

I tossed my shirt and pants in the trash after making a mental note on my expense account. I found fresh underwear and a button-down in my bag, shimmied painfully into a pair of jeans, and then delicately dragged a comb through my remaining hair. I didn't have another jacket, so I still smelled like bruised fruit, but if anybody complained I'd open a window. As I finished packing, I took a quick look around the room and realized it *was* quite a mess. If I really did have to pay for the repairs, plus the ER bill, then I'd dug quite a hole for myself. I'd already blown through the advance money, so if I had any hopes of coming out ahead, or at least breaking even, I'd have to stay in my employer's good graces. Which meant I should give her a call before I boarded the bus. I had no clue why she'd even want her bastard husband back, but she'd paid me to do a job and I should at least let her know the asswipe was still alive.

I tried calling from the room, but they wouldn't give me an outside line unless I left a phone deposit first. Classy joint. I donned my fruit coat and hit the street where I found a pay phone in the shadow of the big elephant's butt. I fumbled with my calling card and got through on my second attempt.

"Hello?" came my boss's foggy voice over the phone.

"Good morning, Mrs. Gardner. This is Frank Rotten," I said, trying to sound professional though I felt like shit. "Sorry to disturb you so early, but I wanted you to know that I found your husband."

"Who's this?" she asked and I heard a rustling in the background.

"Frank Rotten. The detective you hired?"

"You found Billy?" she asked as she finally snapped awake.

"Yes, I did."

"Put him on."

"Well, he's not here right now," I said, wishing I'd taken a moment to rehearse.

"Where is he?"

"I don't know exactly, but—"

"I don't understand. You found him and you let him get away?"

"He had a gun."

"I don't believe it," she said, still sailing on that river in Egypt. "Billy doesn't own a gun."

"Maybe he borrowed it, I don't know," I said, losing what little patience I had left. "He had a gun, he shot me in the leg, he ran away."

"Don't take that tone with me, you little shit. Now put Billy on."

I was about to put the phone back on the hook when I heard another rustling and a muffled exchange, after which the tone of shrill bossiness was replaced by one of husky accommodation.

"Good morning, Mr. Rotten. This is Alison Owen."

Well, no more wondering, I thought to myself. "Good morning, Alison," I said.

"I understand you found Mr. Gardner."

"Yeah, I found him."

"What's this about a gun?"

"Billy Boy wasn't too happy to see me. He had a gun. We tussled, I got shot, he ran off."

"Are you alright?" she asked with apparent sincerity.

"I'll survive, but, you know, this is *not* what I signed on for. Your friend there is deluding herself about that jerkweed husband of hers. He's not off on a lark. He's a total, fucking degenerate."

"She's well aware of his shortcomings, but there are complications. It's been a difficult adjustment," she said quietly. "She's not feeling well this morning." A pause and then, "Did you get a chance to talk with him?"

"I talked to him, but I don't think I made an impression. He's not a good listener. Say, whose baby is it, anyway?" I asked impulsively.

Major pause. Something covered the phone at her end, and, I must confess, I imagined it pressed against her breast. I listened closely and thought I heard a heartbeat, and then she was back on the line. "Who told you?" she asked, sans the accommodating tone.

"Hey, I'm a detective. This is what I do," I said as a wave of fatigue washed over me. "Forget I asked. It doesn't really matter, does it?"

"I assume Billy knows now."

"He knows, but I'm not sure he believes."

"That won't matter much in the long run either."

"Is that what you wanted to talk to him about?"

"That's no concern of yours," she said and I could tell our friendship was fading; but even with an edge, her voice sounded sweet, and I was not inclined to argue.

"Whatever," I said. "Listen, the bus is pulling out soon and I need to be on it. You guys'll get a full report when I get back."

"You think Billy's on his way home?"

"I have no idea what his plans are, and I don't much care. He talked about taking another crack at the tables, but the police are looking for him. Who knows what he'll do. He actually won a ton of money, before he lost most of it back."

"God, I wish he'd go away for good," she said with a sigh.

"I'll be in touch," I said and hung up the receiver, exhausted by the permutations.

I leaned against the phone stand and let the quiet of the off-season streets soothe my rankled nerves, and then I limped around to Lucy's other end and sat on the bulkhead. There we were, a palatial pachyderm and a battered detective sitting on the edge of America, staring out to sea. "Why all the tap dancing?" I asked the out-sized elephant as the sun shone brightly on the deserted beach. "Why not just tell the bozo, 'I like girls. I want a baby. You're outta here?'"

Old Lucy understood the rhetorical nature of my inquiry and offered no reply. And even if she had an answer, she wasn't about to share it with a shoobie. I sat a while longer, listening to the gentle lap of the waves, and then I left Lucy with her thoughts and limped off in search of the oft-mentioned continental breakfast.

EIGHTEEN

One For My Baby

I thought I'd take another crack at chatting up Terry, now that I'd cleaned up a bit, but she was heavily involved dishing out danish. I snagged a cheese and a cup of joe and hung around the lobby until people started looking my way and whispering. I knew it wouldn't be long before someone came up and asked me about last night, so I left the lobby and wandered back through the courtyard to the pool deck. The pool still held water though it hadn't been cleaned in a while. There was a sun deck above the pump house, and there were a few lounge chairs scattered about so I took my continental up there and lounged.

Yesterday's clouds had blown out to sea, and the sun was growing warm. The ocean shimmered and sparkled, and boats bobbed here and there. A few more degrees, and a little less breeze, and we'd have an Indian summer on our hands. This was the stuff that must have attracted people to the Shore in the first place, and if that wasn't enough, then you were just being greedy. Why the need to gamble? And why here? Casinos should be built in places where no one but gamblers would want to go, like over a landfill or in the middle of a toxic waste dump. It was all about easy money. Like I knew what I was talking about, but it seemed that everything these days had to be easy—grades, jobs, relationships. No one expected to encounter any resistance or adversity. "What do we want?" "Fill in the blank." "When do we want it?" "Now!" Maybe that's what all this baby business was about; it was easy. Not easy to raise one, but easy enough to make, with tools you'll find around the house. Used to be, or so I've been told, people had to earn their status symbols. Back in the day, it was washing machines, weedless lawns, and color TVs. Then came BMWs and beach houses. Now it seemed to be babies. One more commodity to bolster self-esteem acquired on credit. But what a fucking mess when the bill comes due!

I was surprising myself. It wasn't like me to wax philosophic. Must have been the knock on the head. I was enjoying it though, at least until I heard big diesel engines rumbling to life and I imagined myself left behind, philosophizing. The thought that I might "find" Gardner again roused me to action. I limped back to my room, grabbed my bag, and stood first in line to board the bus. Unfortunately, Old Sy fell in right behind me. It was clear he considered us co-conspirators and expected to be briefed. We took our same seats, but I sat back and closed my eyes in an effort to blow him off. Old Sy, however, was not to be denied.

"Hey, fella. You shouldn't sleep with a knock on the head like that," he advised from across the aisle.

"Wake me up if I start to twitch," I said without looking his way.

"You ever find that guy you were looking for?" he asked, and I knew he wasn't about to give up. "The schoolteacher?"

"It was all a big misunderstanding," I said, turning to him with a smile. "Guy wasn't missing after all. He was there the whole time." Sy looked doubtful. "Hey, wherever you go, there you are, right?" I added and now Sy looked pissed. With any luck he'd ignore me the whole way home.

I caught Terry's eye when she climbed aboard, but she flashed a smart-assed smile and settled in beside Earl. So be it. I didn't mind being by myself. The last thing I wanted to listen to was more advice. I waved goodbye to Lucy as we pulled out and then tried to get settled myself, but couldn't find a position which took the pressure off my head and leg at the same time. Every little bump, every short stop for a traffic light seemed to stretch the stitches. When we finally hit the highway, I found a spot that let me stabilize enough to rest my eyes. And rest them I did, despite the doctor's warnings.

I didn't mean to fall asleep. I was simply reviewing the weekend's events and feeling good about the way I'd handled the case so far, but eventually I drifted off to . . . *Dreamland*, a luxurious casino/hotel in the *All-New* Atlantic City! I was back in town for a private detectives' convention, and all the heavy hitters were there—the Spades, your Rockfords, some Marlowes. We were all in the ballroom, swapping war stories, waiting for the show to start. The *Fabulous* Dancing Camcorders were supposed to be headlining, but an Elvis impersonator announced that the group had lost its booking when two of the dancers dropped out to have babies. Another decided to go to law school and one really wanted to direct. Two others renounced the life, moved in together, and founded a twelve-step program for recovering tape abusers. Then the real Pat Cooper came out and told jokes I didn't understand, though Rockford was rolling in the aisle. Pat was followed by Bob Seagull and the Silver Bud Band who played "Mandy's on the Run in a Chevy Truck", over, and over, and over . . .

"Frank, wake up," said Terry as she none-too-gently shook my shoulder.

"Say what?" I responded groggily.

"You were starting to twitch," she said, leaning over the empty seat, emphasizing her assets. "Next you'll be foaming at the mouth."

"No, I'll be alright," I said though my head throbbed.

"I just need some water to take my pills."

"Just a minute," she said, then walked back to her seat, and returned with a plastic Evian bottle which she offered to me.

"Thanks," I said and then she sat in the empty seat beside me. I took my pills and handed her back her water. I was pleasantly surprised when she made no immediate move back to the front of the bus. It seemed the jury was still out on me. She was trying to decide how much of a blockhead I really was.

"How long was I out?" I asked.

"About three hours."

"Pretty wild weekend, huh?" I said after a lull.

"For you, at least."

"What, you don't like the casinos?"

"Too many horny old men hitting on me," she said, and I hoped I wasn't included in that group.

"You do any other tours?"

"We start ski trips to the Poconos in a few weeks, depending on the weather."

"I've never been skiing. Maybe I'll give it a try."

"You need *two* good legs for that, Frank."

"Oh, this is just a flesh wound," I said, patting my thigh and wincing. "I'll be ready to go next weekend."

"You still don't look too good," she said to slow me down.

"I haven't had much to eat lately," I said. "I think I'll feel better after I get some food in me." And look better too, I hoped.

"We're stopping soon for dinner," she said as she stood.

"I'll see you later," I said, and with that she walked back to her seat. The poor girl couldn't make up her mind. Sy looked my way as if to say, "I told you so," and I looked out the window at cow country and cars passing by.

I did what I often do on the road. I wondered where the hell everybody was going. At any one time, there were millions of people who were neither here nor there. They were en route, underway, between things. And as soon as they get somewhere, they start thinking about heading back. Always afraid they're missing out on something. I figured I was missing a Steelers game, some sleep, and a few meals, and I started thinking that Terry had missed the mark on dinner. Who ate this early? Apparently, the Amish do. At least on Sunday. Before long we were leaving the Turnpike and following the hex signs to Zimmerman's Harvest House where we filed off and queued up for the "Plain Person's 'All-You-Can-Eat' Harvest Buffet"—a cornucopia of fatty meats, mashed root vegetables, homemade relishes, biscuits, and the biggest bowl of succotash I have seen in my short life, with gravy over everything. And something soft and brown for dessert. Washed down with whole milk. I could hear my arteries clogging as I circled the table, and the sight of all that glistening meat made me feel a little queasy. I opted for a bowl of mashed turnips and a cup of tea which I downed quickly before wandering outside for some air.

Unfortunately, the air wasn't all that fresh since ours was not the only bus left idling on the lot. Zimmerman's was something of a Plain Person's "South of the Border," offering a wide range of tourist attractions including gift shop, miniature golf, and buggy rides around the big parking lot for five bucks a pop. I was feeling antsy and at loose ends, so I paid my fare and let myself be lulled by the unrushed clip-clop of horses' hooves. With the Harvest House behind us, it was easy to gaze out over the adjacent fields and imagine that things hadn't changed much in the past hundred years. What would it be like to lead a "simple" life? I wondered. Would I be happier if the burden of choice were lifted? Would it be easier to get up every day with rules to follow, knowing what was expected of me? Did the Amish accept applications? I was about to pay for a second circuit so I could quiz the plain-person driver when I noticed some of our group filing back to the bus. Then Terry emerged and shot me a sour look, and I reluctantly left the simple life behind. I stopped and stood by the tour guide's side as the buffet-stuffed excursionists groaned aboard. Terry was doing her best to ignore me, but I decided to roll the dice.

"So, whatta ya think?" I said, shifting my weight to my good leg. "Maybe the two of us could get together some time, when we get back to the city. Go out to eat, maybe catch a movie?"

She turned and looked me square in the eye. "I don't date flakes," she said.

"Flakes? Who says I'm a flake?"

"You're off the wall, Frank, all over the map," was her assessment.

"Aw, what's this? One buggy ride makes me a flake? I've got my own business, a car, I'm housebroken. It's not like I'm asking you to marry me."

"Forget it, Frank," she said, holding firm. "It's time to go."

I didn't have the strength to argue so I boarded the bus and retook my seat. Sy smiled silently to say he'd seen me get shot down. I scowled his way then stared out the window. She'll be easy to forget, I told myself, and, really, there wasn't much to remember. No kiss to build a dream on, no bells I never heard ringing. I guess I didn't look like much of a catch from where she sat. Just another horn toad hopping by. I was peeved for a bit, but once we hit the open road, I let myself be soothed by the hum of big tires heading home.

NINETEEN

Let's Face the Music and Dance

Unfortunately, that particular set of wheels didn't make it all the way. The damn bus blew a gasket, and we were stuck by the side of the road while a back-up was dispatched from Breezewood, the infamous "Town of Motels." I'd gotten stuck there once in a major snowstorm, stranded at one of those motels. It was the loneliest night of my life. I had the feeling that if I fell asleep, I'd just disappear, never wake up. Bye-bye, Frankie, bye-bye. Can't say what triggered that sensation. Just one of those free-floating existential interludes that I wasn't eager to repeat. No *Twilight Zone* reruns for me, thank you. Luckily, we wouldn't be heading into town. Unluckily, there'd been a major pile-up on I-70 which delayed our relief even longer. And so, we waited, for hours, each in his own way. The Vinnies slept and smoked; the Marlas' big hair drooped; Sy and his wife quietly snored. Terry chatted with Earl and kept a close eye on a quarrelsome couple who'd lost a bundle playing blackjack. They noisily debated strategy—he claimed he'd been counting cards. When she replied that he couldn't count his change at McDonald's, he threatened to walk home alone. She maintained he couldn't find his way home from work most days, and Terry couldn't dissuade him from setting off along the shoulder.

"Go get lost in the woods, ya stupid shit," yelled the unworried wife to her departing spouse. Thankfully, or not, the back-up arrived before he'd gone fifty yards. The loving couple was reunited aboard the new bus and our trek continued.

We finally arrived back in Pittsburgh just after seven. We were only about two hours behind schedule, though it felt like forever. Nobody wasted much time saying, "I'll see you later," but Terry surprised me by suggesting that I give her a call. At work, and only after my hair grew back. Poor girl couldn't make up her mind.

My Toyota wagon was where I'd left it, and as I slid behind the wheel, I almost felt like I had a future. Hope springs eternal, like a noxious weed. Cars were leaving the lot, and headlights swept the seat as I sat momentarily lost in thought. I only snapped out of my reverie when I realized that a pair of those lights were heading straight for me. I hurriedly coaxed the old wagon into gear but, before I could move, the other car broke hard, turned into a skid, and slid into my front end. Welcome back, Rotten. I sat stupefied as an enraged Alison Owen emerged from her Saab and raced around to my door, which she proceeded to kick several times.

"Fucking-A!" I shouted. "Get a grip!" But as I struggled my way out, she started smacking me.

"You bastard," she said, enraged. Whap! Whap! "You sold me out." Whap! Whap!

"What the hell are you talking about? And stop smacking me," I said as I pushed her back against her fender.

"Mona wanted me out of Lizzie's life, and you sold yourself to the highest bidder. Fucking whore!" she said and stepped forward to smack me again, but I blocked her hand.

"What's this all about? Have you seen Gardner?" I asked, but she only laughed. "Where is he?"

"Don't play dumb. You know damn well where he is, or will be soon, and you helped it happen."

"I don't know what the hell you're talking about," I said in my defense, and I didn't. She moved closer again, and I raised my arm to block the blow, but she switched tacks.

"All you dicks hang together," she seethed as she kneed me in the groin.

I slumped against my door to catch my breath, and she drove off, leaving parts from both cars clattering on the asphalt. Earl trotted over to see if I was okay. Thankfully, Terry was dropping some stuff off at the travel office and hadn't been a witness. I assured the burly bus driver that I could make it home alright, and, though he seemed doubtful, he left me on my own.

Should I have seen this coming? What had even happened? I couldn't decide, and the more I thought about it, the more my head hurt, so I stopped. I might as well have been in love for all the grief this case was causing me. I took a moment to collect my car parts, then slid back behind the wheel, and drove home.

The drive wasn't long at that hour on a Sunday, but long enough for my body to start shutting down. After parking on a side street, I focused on husbanding enough energy to climb the stairs to my apartment without collapsing. One step at a time, I told myself as I gimped down the street. Alas, I was so fixed on reaching my front door that I failed to notice the pearl gray Phantom idling at the curb, until Mona's double-wide driver physically blocked my path. So close, yet so far.

"You've got to be kidding me?" I said as the driver used one meaty paw to guide me to the car, and the other to open the rear door.

"Good evening, Mister Rotten," came the oddly chipper rasp from the rear seat. "Won't you join me?"

"Can't this wait? I'm really not in the mood."

"This won't take long," she said as she took stock of my physical condition. "Viktor can assist you if you need help."

"I think I can make it," I said after a pause, suspicious of the type of assistance Viktor might provide.

"You look like hell, young man," she said almost sympathetically as I gently folded myself onto the rear seat, "So I'll get straight to the point. Did you find Mister Gardner?"

I was fully aware of the need to focus, but I was running on fumes. I could feel an out-of-body experience coming on. "You have anything to drink?" I asked.

Mona flashed a look of frustration, but she unsnapped the seat back in front of her and retrieved a bottle of Perrier. It was even chilled. "Now about William?" she asked again as I swigged the sparkling water.

"Yes, I found him."

"And?"

"He wasn't happy to see me, hence my current condition, and he didn't seem inclined to take your offer."

"The money wasn't enough?"

"I don't think the amount was the problem. He doesn't trust that you'll deliver."

"Where is he now?"

"You haven't heard from him then?"

"I have not," she said. "Is he home?"

"I have no idea where he is, but I doubt he's headed home. The police are looking for him. Have you talked to your daughter?"

"I have, but we have markedly different perspectives on the situation, and the circumstances have changed somewhat."

I suspected she knew her daughter was pregnant, but I was beyond caring how that would play out, and I was tired of tap-dancing. Neither one of us was willing to give up much, and the only thing I cared about was getting to bed. Since that wasn't happening, I decided it was time to talk turkey.

"I'd love to sit and chat some more," I said, "But I really need some rest. I'm sure you're not happy with the outcome, but I made the offer, and we had a deal."

She glared at me icily, and I could sense an internal calculus at work. She was wondering whether the money was worth the trouble I might cause if she simply blew me off. Now, I was probably overestimating my ability to cause her any grief, but a thousand bucks didn't mean much to a woman like Ramona Baldwin Taft, so after a long moment, she reached into the Coach bag at her feet, pulled out a slender manila envelope, and handed it over.

"Pleasure doing business," I said with a smile as I turned to unfold myself from the seat.

"Watch your step moving forward, Mister Rotten," she said evenly. "I will brook no meddling in my affairs."

I didn't care for her tone, but I was flat out of snappy comebacks, plus I needed Viktor's help getting out of the car, so I kept my mouth shut. Meeting adjourned, I stood stupidly on the sidewalk and waved as the Rolls receded into the night.

With considerable effort, I made my way into my building and began the long slow climb to my humble abode. No light shone under Trudy's door which was just as well since I'd forgotten her saltwater taffy. I smiled as I crossed my threshold and snuck a quick peek in the manila envelope. The money was all there. And, as an added bonus, Des was out working, or carousing, so embarrassing explanations about my physical condition could wait till morning. There was nothing to eat in the fridge, and I wasn't about to cook, but Des had left me a few beers, so I popped a Rock—another violation of doctor's orders—and sat at my desk. I had no intentions of opening mail at that hour, but my answering machine was flashing furiously, and I could listen without much effort, so I hit the button and sat back.

The first message was from Mona, on Saturday morning, warning me not to get "too cute." The second was from my client, earlier in the day, insisting on a call as soon as I arrived home, "whatever the hour." The last, from Alison, was basically a preamble to the message she'd delivered in person in the parking lot. What had I done to offend that woman? I was totally toast at that point and way ready for bed, but a quick tally of my expenses told me I was still in the hole, even with Mona's bonus. I couldn't afford to alienate my client till we'd settled, so I beat the dead horse and dialed her number. She picked up on the first ring.

"Yes, where are you?" Miz Liz asked in a rush, clearly expecting someone else.

"I'm home," I said. "I just got in."

"Who is this?"

"Frank Rotten. You asked me to call."

"Shit, I don't have time for this now."

"You left a message. You said to call—"

"Thank you, Mr. Rotten, your services are no longer required. Send me a bill." And with that she hung up the phone.

To be sure, that's exactly what I wanted, to get paid without having to go through with the whole dog-and-pony show. And yet, nobody likes getting blown off, and now I was curious. What the fuck was going on? I called her back right away, but she let her machine pick up. I called three times in quick succession, but I couldn't goad her into answering, so I gave it up. My body said enough, so I gave it all up. I locked the door, finished my beer, and crawled off to bed.

TWENTY

Same As It Ever Was

I dreamed again. The private eyes' convention was over. Spade and Marlowe had faded into the fog, and Rockford was combing the beach. I was hitchhiking out of town on one of those lonely causeways that crossed the marshland. My reunited parents drove by in an old Ford Falcon, and I hid behind a billboard. Alison Owen tried to run me down in her Saab. A pearl gray Phantom cruised past. The pony-tailed chauffeur grinned and waved, while Liz and Mona argued in the back. A tour bus to Easy Street rumbled through with Earl at the wheel. He kept his eyes on the road and his hands upon the wheel, as Terry stroked his thigh and unbuttoned her blouse. I was left sucking diesel fumes. Then nothing. The traffic died and I curled up under some shrubbery to sleep. I was wakened in the faint light of early morn by someone rustling through my knapsack. I raised my head to see that the rustler was Des who was rummaging through my bureau drawers.

"What the hell're you doing?" I mumbled groggily.

"You owe me some socks," he said. "Shit, man, what the hell happened to your head?"

"I fell," I replied vaguely. "What time is it?"

"About eight. Are you alright?" he asked with a look of concern. "You don't look too good."

"I'll be fine," I assured him though I had my doubts. "What're you up to anyway?"

"I just dropped in for a few things. Yolanda's waiting in the car."

"Shit, I'm not losing a roommate, am I?"

"Don't worry, it's strictly physical," he promised. "It won't last."

The phone rang and Des rushed down to pick it up before the machine did. "It's Trudy," he called up the stairs.

I stumbled to the landing and sat on the top step. "Tell her I'll call back," I said and yawned.

Des talked with Trudy a minute more, then a horn sounded outside, and he hung up and moved to the door with his bag. "Hey, how much I win at roulette?" he asked.

"You're lookin' at it. How was the party Saturday night?"

"Awesome. Stop by the Row later, I've got details," he said and the horn sounded again. He looked at me closely. "You should take it easy today. You really do look like crap," he added, and then he was gone.

I thought about it. Taking it easy. Then I thought about bonus money, my bills, and agitated crazy people running around, and I decided I should try to wrap things up as soon as possible.

The hospital had given me a supply of disposable shower caps, so I donned one and wrapped a trash bag around my leg and took a half-assed shower. I dressed gingerly, then brewed a pot of coffee, and called my client. Again, with the answering machine. I called several times more while I opened my mail, all with the same result, so I finally decided to slap a bill together and run it out there myself. Hand deliver the sucker, check the lay of the land, maybe get my face slapped. As I checked the mirror to straighten my tie, I could see why Des had advised me to take it easy. With pallid skin, racoon eyes, greasy hair, and a lumpy head bandage, I was not a pretty picture. But at least I didn't stink, and this was not a social call. I wouldn't be staying long.

Even missing the morning rush, it took a good twenty minutes to get out to Fox Hollow, which was almost long enough for me to change my mind and turn back to bed. When at last I *did* arrive, I found I was not the first to come calling. Mona's Rolls was already parked in the drive, though Viktor was nowhere to be seen. I pulled in behind the Phantom and approached the front door feeling somewhat exposed. I rang the bell, waited a few minutes, and then rang again. I was thinking seriously about just dropping the bill in the letter box when the door swung open and there stood Billy "Big-As-Life" Gardner, looking sober and tweedy and right at home. Fuckin'-A. No wonder Alison had been so pissed.

"What the fuck?" I said softly, blinking stupidly. Then I couldn't suppress a smile, and added, "You stinking son of a bitch."

An awkward, silent moment passed before Gardner muttered, "Wait here," and closed the door.

He left me cooling my heels for close to five minutes, ample time to recall all the indignities I'd endured over the weekend. I figured the bastard was blowing me off, so I started pounding the door with a balled fist. Almost immediately, Gardner reappeared, wearing a tight smile and holding a buff-colored business envelope.

"Sorry I can't ask you in," he said as he stepped onto the stoop, pulling the door closed behind him. "Liz is not feeling well."

I was dumbstruck. Waiting on the stoop, I had begun to doubt what I'd seen. It wasn't so much that he was *there*, he was just so matter of fact about it, and it made no sense.

"What the fuck are you doing here?" I finally said, repeating myself, but recovering some attitude.

"I live here," he said as his smile widened.

"I need to see your wife. I have her final bill."

He snatched the bill disdainfully and handed me his fat envelope. "This should more than cover it," he said.

I took a quick look and caught flashes of Franklin. Many smiling Benjamins. "I want to see my client," I said.

"It's not gonna happen, kid. Nothing personal." When I continued to stand there, mouth agape, he felt compelled to ask, "How's your head?"

"She know what a total sleaze you are?"

"Liz and I have known each other for twenty years."

"She know the police are after you?"

"If the police were after me, they'd have called already."

"She know about you and her mother?" I said, stopping him short.

I sensed a fog was lifting. Billy was just remembering some of the things he'd said at the Shore. "She doesn't need to know," he said with an edge in his voice. "And she wouldn't believe you if you told her."

"Maybe we should find out."

Gardner snatched the envelope back and gave me a hard, classroom glare. "Long ago and far away, sport. Quit while you're ahead," he said and then shoved the cash back at me.

Old Bill knew something about sleaze alright. He knew I wanted that money more than I needed to tell his secret. I stashed the cash in my jacket pocket, but I couldn't let him off that easy. "So how much do *you* know, old man?" I said with a smirk. "You know whose baby it is?"

He started with that classroom look again, then smiled, and shook his head. "You're a piece of work, kid," he said with a chuckle. "Hell, the father doesn't matter. Liz went to a sperm bank. The records are sealed. It will be *my* baby, our little bundle of joy."

Now it was my turn to stop short. I looked around at the Rolls and then back at Billy. "I can't believe the old lady's buying this crap," I said, shaking my head.

"Not buying, selling. This was mostly her idea. She got a glimpse of the future while I was away, saw who'd be sleeping in my bed," he said with a fairy tale flourish. "And so, I'm being rehabilitated. I'm going back to school. With Mona's help, I just may be a principal someday."

"You're not worth the effort."

"Maybe not, but life has a way of limiting options," he said with a sad smile. "If you can't face the truth, you make shit fit. Liz always wanted a kid, and Mona wants someone to leave her money to. That leaves Allie out." He paused. "I could do worse," he concluded.

His talent for rationalization left me momentarily speechless. "How do you do it?" I asked at length.

"What's that?"

"How do you live with yourself?"

"Take a good look, kid," he said and smiled. "This could be you someday."

There was just enough doubt in me to think it might be possible. I couldn't handle it. Something snapped and I had to take a shot and show him he was wrong. I cocked my fist and Gardner pressed against the door, but before I could follow through, Viktor had my arm pretzeled behind me.

Where the hell had *he* come from? Billy smiled again and waved as the business-like hardbody stuffed me in my car. The house door closed, and Billy was back in the bosom of his family, back where he belonged.

"You best be running along," Viktor said as he patted the roof of my wagon.

"Fuck you," I said scowling, but I did as I was told.

I closed and locked my door and then sat for a moment, a little disappointed that I was giving up so easy. I thought briefly of the baby, and all the kids Gardner would be back teaching, but it was too sick to contemplate. I screamed a few obscenities and then leveled my client's lamppost as I backed out of her drive. I flipped Viktor the bird and sped away in a funk, barely making it around the second bend before being run off the road by Alison Owen's battered Saab. I don't think she even saw me, but I'd seen the hard-set look in her eyes, and I considered heading back to the house. As I reached for the gear shift though, I felt the weight of the buff-colored envelope in my pocket, and I simply straightened the car on the shoulder. I pulled the envelope out and inventoried its contents—fifty fresh Franklins, and two weathered tickets to Woodstock. Not a fortune, but even after expenses, my best payday since I'd been in the business. I smiled and felt a tingling wave of self-satisfaction ripple through me, and then my stomach clenched as two gunshots sounded in the near distance behind me.

Fuck, fuck, fuck, I muttered to myself as my mind raced. *Think, Frank.*

I closed my eyes and lowered my head to the steering wheel, but thinking didn't help a bit. In my mind's eye, I saw the fallen lamppost, the ghostly Phantom, and the walkway to the Gardners' front door. I saw a blood-stained stoop and a half-opened door, but the scene was eerily still. The soundtrack had paused; the players had left the stage. I opened my eyes before I could imagine anything more. I knew there'd be a body back there. I didn't know whose, but I convinced myself there was nothing I could do about it. I put the envelope back in my pocket and drove thoughtlessly home as sirens swirled in the autumn air.

TWENTY-ONE

Wouldn't It Be Loverly?

Did I do the wrong thing? Maybe. I don't know. What's the right thing to do when there's nothing to be done? I waited at home all day for a call that never came and then went down to the Row around happy hour where Casey was there to greet me.

"You look like shit, Frank," was her appraisal as she served me a beer. "You should think about sticking with scene sketches for a while."

"I intend to. This one wore me out."

"You found your guy, though?"

"I did that. A bit of serendipity, but I flushed him out, and he found his own way home."

"That's what your client was paying you for, right? You got the job done. That's what matters."

"I suppose," I said, but I couldn't shake my final vision of a grinning Billy Gardner. "You ever have second thoughts about stuff you did on the job?" I asked the ex-cop.

"There's a few things I might do differently if they came up again," she said after thinking a bit. "But I learned not to beat myself up too bad. You'll never figure everything out, and there's always some fresh hell to face."

Casey was called off to consult with another customer, but I didn't sit solo for long. Des arrived and told me all about the party, and I made up stories about my bandaged head, searching for the best fit. Trudy dropped in briefly and gave me a warm, welcome-back hug, before scolding me for being so reckless. I promised to be more careful moving forward, then I bought a round for the house, fed the jukebox, and ignored the evening news. I played all my favorite tunes, even sang along with a few, but my feet couldn't find the rhythm. Des left with Yolanda, and not long after, I settled my tab, thanked Casey for her counsel, and limped home alone.

The next day, I tied up a few loose ends and started stitching together a new routine, though I couldn't avoid the news forever. There had been bloodshed back at the Gardners' house, but no one came close to dying. Both Billy and the bodyguard had been nicked in the thigh, treated in the ER, and released. Either Alison's aim was off, or she was sending a message of some sort. Maybe the sperm donor had an identity after all. In any case, no charges were ever filed. Mona hired some serious spin doctor, and it was apparently all an accident. Whatta ya know? Alison had been returning a target pistol she'd borrowed from Liz. She hadn't realized the gun was loaded, or that the safety was off. The exchange was fumbled, and two poor guys nearly lost their balls. At least mine had only been bruised.

Nobody came looking for *me*, and I made no effort to follow up, although I did think about giving Ann Deaver a call. Thought it might be nice to hear her voice and get her take on all this crap. But then I realized Billy was probably back at work, and she might be a bit disillusioned right now, and I was in no position to offer any comfort. Pearls of wisdom were decidedly not in my repertoire. I couldn't say what I had learned, if anything, so I simply swept it from my head. I banked the Benjamins, reframed the ducats, and turned the page. Filed all the details away for future reference and rumination, but no time too soon, if ever.

My hair eventually grew back, and I bought a camcorder. The surveillance van will have to wait. I finished that scene sketch for Karen Stanley, and she promised more work, for which I was grateful. I got my wagon's front end fixed, and, after several calls and a few drive-bys, Terry finally agreed to go out with me. Nothing fancy, just a movie and a bite to eat, but it was nice. We had a good time. No dancing yet, but if we ever settle on a song, she's promised to teach me how.

ABOUT THE AUTHOR

Michael Glennon was born and raised in Upper Darby PA and currently resides along the Jersey Shore. He attended Antioch College and has worked a variety of day jobs (kindergarten teacher, desk clerk, insurance adjustor) since graduating. His stories have appeared in The Red Herring Mystery Magazine, Horror Sleaze Trash, and Short-Story.me. *Song and Dance* is the inaugural entry in the Frank Rotten series.